only for a night

THE LICK SERIES
BOOK 1

NAIMA SIMONE

This book is a work of fiction. Names, characters, places, and incidents are the product of the author's imagination or are used fictitiously. Any resemblance to actual events, locales, or persons, living or dead, is coincidental.

Copyright © 2016 by Naima Simone. All rights reserved, including the right to reproduce, distribute, or transmit in any form or by any means. For information regarding subsidiary rights, please contact the Publisher.

Entangled Publishing, LLC
2614 South Timberline Road
Suite 109
Fort Collins, CO 80525
Visit our website at www.entangledpublishing.com.

Scorched is an imprint of Entangled Publishing, LLC.

Edited by Tracy Montoya
Cover design by Liz Pelletier
Cover art from iStock

Manufactured in the United States of America

First Edition May 2016

To Gary. 143.

Chapter One

Sex not only sold—it sold like a motherfucker.

Rion Ward leaned against the glass top of the bar and sipped from the one glass of liquor he permitted himself every night before the festivities kicked into high gear. The smooth, smoke-and-caramel flavor of the twenty-three-year-old Pappy Van Winkle bourbon slid over his tongue like a benediction. Drinking the Kentucky whiskey might be seen as treason in his part of the country, the home of Sam Adams, but fuck it. The shit was good.

He surveyed the shadowed, cavernous room. Satisfaction beat within him, as warm and bright as the bourbon. Exposed brick walls lent character to the converted warehouse while two long, wide glass and chrome bars dominated either side of the building. Strategically placed halogen lights illuminated the bars, the glass-enclosed balconies, the dance floor already growing more packed with people, and the stage. High tables dotted the space around the dance floors, and long, leather couches resided in shadowed corners and alcoves.

In the 1800s, this brick building in Boston's Leather

District might have once been used for leather manufacturing, but today it housed Lick, the city's hottest and most exclusive aphrodisiac club. Since its opening a year ago, Lick had quickly become the hottest place to party thanks to the patronage of sports figures, actors and actresses, musicians, and other celebrities. The bottom level of the building provided music spun by the country's most popular and in-demand DJs; premium, top-shelf alcohol; dancing; VIP lounges; and the best time to be had in Boston.

But on the upper levels in the loft-style apartments…Lick delivered the ultimate—and kinkiest—fantasies. Bondage. Spanking. Domination and submission. Voyeurism. Role play. The club provided a private, safe, and luxurious place for well-vetted members to indulge in the most carnal and dirty side of their needs and imaginations. Whatever sexual aphrodisiac stimulated or excited a person's desires, Lick catered to them—for an exorbitant annual fee.

Not bad for three ex-members of the Irish mob.

And a far cry from the world of extortion, weapons trafficking, and murder they used to live in. Now they dealt in kink…not blood.

So Lick was more than a business. It was his, Sasha's, and Killian's redemption.

And Rion guarded it jealously.

"Rion."

Sasha Merchant, one of his best friends and one-third owner of Lick, leaned against the bar railing next to Rion. Before Sasha could turn to the bartender, a tumbler of vodka appeared beside his elbow. Nodding his thanks to the pretty brunette and ignoring the I'm-down-to-fuck invitation in her smile, Sasha picked up the drink and fixed his eerily bright blue and gray gaze on him. He reminded Rion of the wolf Sasha's homeland was known for. The pale blond hair cut close to his head; slanted, exotic eyes; harsh facial structure;

and big, wide-shouldered frame declared his Russian heritage.

"Hey, Sasha. Everything okay?"

He grunted, sipping from his glass. "Not exactly. Caught a guy dealing out of the bathroom last night. Said he's an O'Bannon."

Fuck.

Rion, Sasha, and Killian had decided to go straight two years ago, but getting out of the O'Bannon gang—one of Boston's Irish mobs—had been hell. Even being the son of Darry Ward, the infamous mob hitman and enforcer, hadn't held any sway with the boss, Jamie Hughes. Blood had been spilled, and… He clenched his jaw. The bottom line was they got out…even if the how of it haunted him in the middle of the night.

And damn if the O'Bannons were going to worm their way into the dream he, Sasha, and Killian had sacrificed so much for. Or drag them back into that life.

"Let him stay. For now," Rion said, voice grim. "And with the reminder that he keeps his ass clean. I don't care if he's an O'Bannon. While he's here in our house, he follows our rules. And that includes no dealing." So far, they hadn't experienced any trouble with their former gang. So far. He doubted the O'Bannons were making a push on them, but they would also be fools to not be prepared and ready to defend what was theirs.

Sasha's lips thinned into a flat line, and after several seconds, he nodded.

"Anything else?" Rion downed the last of the bourbon and set the glass on the bar behind him. He glanced down at his watch. Eleven o'clock on a Friday night. Still fairly early down here, with people pouring through the club's doors and crowding around the bars and on the dance floors.

"Yeah, one more thing." Sasha frowned down into his drink, his fingers clenching and unclenching around the thick glass. When he glanced up, wariness darkened his wolf eyes, and unease tripped down Rion's spine. If Sasha was nervous, then they all needed to buy fleece and fur-lined drawers because hell was experiencing a cold snap.

"What?" Rion pressed.

Another beat of hesitation. "Harper Shaw is here."

Fuck. He shouldn't have asked.

• • •

Mission for tonight.

Booty call.

Wait. Did people even say that anymore? What were they calling it now? Hook up? Getting ass?

God. Harper Shaw sighed, sipping on her virgin rum-and-Coke…which, okay, was just a Coke. *I'm astronomically bad at this.*

What had she expected? That once she stepped into the popular club, all her inhibitions and nerves would fly off like Britney Spears' panties? She snorted. If only.

Not that the stark yet elegant and sexy decor didn't inspire a person to let her freak flag fly. Even if just for a little wave. The large, framed, black-and-white photographs dotting the exposed brick walls had her blinking, then flushing, and in desperate need of a fan: A bed with tangled sheets and pillows with indentations as if lovers had just climbed out. Couples in silhouette, their bodies straining toward one another. The moon shining over the dark, mysterious water of Boston Harbor. Two hands—one masculine, the other slim and feminine—entwined, tightened around the other.

Rion's work. There were no name plates to reveal the identity of the photographer, but she didn't need them. In her soul, she recognized his sensitivity and sensuality in the beauty that radiated from them.

She contemplated the rest of the room. The black and chrome tables and chairs; the wide, red and dark blue couches along the walls and tucked into corners. The glass balconies with crimson drapes and gorgeous staff in tight leather pants and blue silk halter tops or white shirts… Yes, sexy.

But so damn intimidating.

Stop it.

She curled her fingers into a tight fist as if she would use it to fight the urge to scurry back to the safe bolt hole she called a house. Two years, damn it. It'd been two years since Terrance's death. Three since Carlie's, the precious baby she'd lost, miscarrying at seven-and-a-half months. She briefly closed her eyes, and the bite of fingernails digging into her palm helped beat back the throb of pain in her chest. The thought of Terrance and Carlie no longer buckled her knees like it used to, time and grieving having dulled the serrated edges some. Still… She sipped through her straw, the cold, crisp soda distracting her from ambling down that pocked and well-travelled road.

The season for mourning had passed. The support group her mother had insisted Harper attend would've claimed she'd entered the seventh phase of the grieving process. Acceptance. And hope. Not for a man or husband. She'd been there, done that, had the shattered dreams and broken promises littering her heart to prove it. Screw the T-shirt.

No, tonight she'd come to Lick—God, she blushed just *thinking* the name—to feel alive again. To break out of the cryogenic state she'd hibernated in for the past three years.

She'd come for sex.

Hot, dirty, black-out-from-orgasm sex that good little Catholic girls from a respectable family shouldn't know about. The kind of sex that had Terrance staring at her as if an alien had snatched his wife's body the first—and only—time she'd dared to whisper her fantasy to him.

Yes, that kind.

And who better to provide it than the man who'd granted her a glimpse of what true need and passion were like before slamming that door shut…and shutting her out. She just had to convince him that a) it was a good idea, and b) she didn't want him to put a ring on it; she just wanted sex.

A shiver quaked through her, the tiny hairs on the nape of her neck rising as if an intent sniper had her in his sights. She inhaled a deep breath, held it, then released it slowly, deliberately… Nada. Didn't do a damn thing for the frantic twisting and knotting in her belly.

Picking up her glass in a trembling hand, she lifted it to her mouth, and shifting on the surprisingly comfortable chrome and leather chair, she covertly scanned the packed room. People mobbed the dance floor, but the sense of being watched—hunted—didn't come from that direction. The itch intensified, as did the fear, anxiety, and…excitement.

The balconies. Nope. The scattering of tables and couches on the far side of the room. Not there, either. The bar…

Oh *God*.

No. Not God. Rion Ward.

Even so, floods of people parted, making way for him, tinges of awe, lust, and envy suffusing their faces. As he stalked closer to her with a sensual glide that triggered her fight-or-flight instinct, wonder and arousal wound through her. Like it always had when she'd been near him in the past. The man was living, breathing, and walking danger…and sex.

She rose, steadying herself with a hand on the table. The sheath dress suddenly seemed too tight, squeezing her so she couldn't even draw in a lungful of air.

Jesus, he was…beautiful.

Nothing of the teen who had first appeared in her life by coming in between her and a couple of bullies existed in the man.

No, that wasn't exactly true.

He still possessed the same slumberous, hooded gaze, the same slashes of dark brows. The black hair appeared as thick, except now those silken waves grazed his razor-sharp cheekbones and the hard line of his jaw instead of falling around his shoulders. The same sensual, full mouth with its hint of cruelty. God, thoughts of that mouth had resulted in more confessions to her priest and Acts of Contrition than she could count. And back then, a dark shadow of a beard hadn't dusted his jaw, chin and surrounded those lips…

In the years that had passed since she'd last seen him, he had become…more. The promise of power and control that had simmered under his skin then, radiated from him now. He wore it with confidence, as easily as he did the immaculately tailored black suit and shirt that draped over his wide shoulders and chest, slender waist, and strong legs. And thighs. Why couldn't she tear her gaze away from the muscles that pressed against the slim cut of his pants with each stride?

She couldn't think. Couldn't grasp and hold onto a single thought as he closed in on her, not halting until scant inches separated them, and she inhaled the wood-and-sex scent of his cologne. A gentleman would've ceded a respectable distance, not invaded her personal space.

But Rion Ward—ex-mob, her former best friend, the first man to break her heart, and star of every secret, illicit fantasy she'd ever dreamed—had never been a gentleman.

For an instant, the hurt and disillusionment from years ago trickled past the fascination and attraction, sparking memories. Painful memories. Of Rion coming to her with a bruised face and knuckles, and Harper, terrified for his life, throwing down an ultimatum—her or the gang. Of her telling Rion that she wanted him, *needed* him, and flinging her heart at his feet, kissing him. And for one blinding moment, of him kissing her back, caressing her breasts and nipples, showing her pleasure for the first time.

Of Rion refusing to leave the mob life behind, and then his terribly gentle rejection, his belief that he wasn't capable of relationships, especially not with her.

Then, finally, of the night she'd informed him about Terrance's marriage proposal...and Rion wishing her happiness and walking away.

"What are you doing here?" The deep, midnight voice sliced through the memories, and she willingly locked the vault on them. His velvet tone slid over her exposed skin like a velvet caress, resonating in her chest, curling in her belly—and lower. She squeezed her thighs together, praying those piercing gray eyes with their thick fringe of almost ridiculously long lashes didn't notice how she shifted on the unfamiliar stilettos that were beginning to pinch her toes. "I asked you a question," he said, the demand silky but no less menacing.

Did it make her depraved or the shameless slut Terrance had called her that the danger embedded in that voice had her sex clenching?

"I-I came here to speak with y-you," she stammered. God, she sounded like an idiot. Forcing her hand to remain by her side and not cover her face in mortification, she tried it again. "I hoped we could talk."

A black eyebrow arched high. "Talk," he enunciated, a corner of his sensual mouth curling into a faintly sardonic sneer. "What could you and I possibly have to *talk* about?"

"I—" She peered over his shoulder, for the first time noticing the blond giant standing behind Rion. A flicker of memory ghosted across her mind, and an image of a tall, lean boy with exotic eyes and an accent superimposed itself over the man. Sasha. Sasha Merchant. A close friend of Rion's. And from the way he loomed behind Rion's shoulder as if protecting his back, he still was. Jerking her regard away from that unwavering and a bit unsettling stare, she returned her attention to Rion. "Would you mind if we... Can we speak in private?"

Without his friend and, oh, hundreds of people, as witnesses. Her reason for searching him out was embarrassing enough. Having an audience for the conversation? Humiliating.

"No."

She reeled back on her death-defying heels, teetering before grabbing the table tighter. "No?" she repeated. Seconds of silence passed between them. Irritation warred with mortification, and she tilted her chin in spite of the heat rushing up her throat and into her face. "That's it? Just no?"

"Yes."

She sighed, exasperated. "Rion..."

"Go home," he interrupted, the order unyielding, hard. Dismissive.

"Rion, please," she murmured, cringing at the plea that crept into her voice.

"Sasha, would you mind escorting her safely to her car?" He turned, again disregarding her without hearing her out.

Anger shoved the hurt aside, surging hot and hard inside her. She'd been dismissed, shelved, or patronized too often in her life. She'd also been mute, opting to remain silent, not rock the boat. Not voice her needs, her wants...her desires. Years ago, he'd been the first person to teach that confessing what—or who—you needed resulted in rejection, humiliation. Terrance had solidified that lesson. Well, that time had passed.

She was tired of living—no, existing—in a cocoon that was supposed to be safe but was really suffocating.

And he didn't get to push her back into that cocoon.

Aiming a dark scowl at Rion, Sasha stepped forward, his hand extended toward her. "Sorry, sweetheart—"

"Wait a minute," she snarled, skirting past Sasha and latching onto Rion's arm, ignoring the sexy flex of muscle beneath her fingers and palm. Rion froze, probably in surprise rather than from her hold. "We were friends for a long time. Too long for you to just toss me aside like a stranger. Okay it's been five years since we've seen one another. You can at least give me five seconds."

Slowly, Rion pivoted, dislodging her hand. Staring up into his lean face with its stark lines and stormy eyes, she shivered. Fear had picked a fine time to remind her of the absolute stupidity of stirring a predator.

Cradling her hand to her chest, she rubbed a thumb over her tingling palm. The palm that had gripped the steel of his arm.

"I'm sorry," she murmured.

"Five seconds." He slid his hands in his pants pockets.

"Thank you." She sighed, relieved. "If we could just—"

"Three," he stated, his tone past bored and veering into catatonic.

"I need you," she blurted. *Damn.* Oh God. Just...*damn.*

His eyes narrowed. "What do you need me for?"

"I can't—" Panic crawling up her throat, she shot a glance at Sasha who didn't even pretend not to be absorbed with the scene playing out before him. "Rion," she whispered.

"Two seconds."

"Damn it. Sex. I need you for sex."

For the first time, Rion lost his stoicism, shock widening his eyes and parting his lips. Beside him, Sasha sounded as if he were being strangled, and her? She squeezed her eyes shut, flames bursting inside her, consuming her in a conflagration of humiliation. *Jesus Christ.* Was death by mortification possible?

"Oh fuck," she groaned.

"Yeah," Rion drawled. "I got that."

Yes. Definitely possible.

Chapter Two

Puppies wrestling. Swan boats floating on a lake. Multi-colored kites swaying in a perfect summer sky.

Rion played the wholesome, innocent images through his mind on an endless loop as he strode into his office, tossing in pictures of frolicking kittens for good measure. Anything to keep his dick from punching a hole through his pants.

Clenching his jaw, he resisted the urge to slam his fists over and over into the nearest wall, instead thrusting his hands into his pockets. Right now, he'd willingly bust up his hands rather than have his chest and gut shredded with the anger and fucking *need* that had no outlet. Unwanted need. Resented need. Five years since he'd last seen her.

She still shouldn't be able to elicit this aching, clawing hunger inside him.

Shouldn't be able to stir memories like old restless ghosts—memories he'd convinced himself were long dead and buried.

Harper Shaw—not Daly; he'd never call her by another man's name—wasn't the one that got away... He'd never had her. She'd offered herself to him, but she'd never truly been his, had always been beyond his reach.

Damn her. The snarl reverberated against the walls of his skull, gaining speed and volume with each pass. *Damn. Her.* For strolling back into his life. For reminding him of what he'd allowed himself to foolishly want, hope for. Dream of. People like him—the son of a mob hitman, a former thief, thug, and worse—didn't dream.

Logically, he acknowledged it had been him who'd inserted the distance between them all those years ago. He should've never gone to her house and tapped on her bedroom window that night. Not with blood on his hands—literally. It should've been a simple collection assignment. But it had gone to hell quick, the guy who'd owed money whipping out a knife and lunging for Rion. But he'd been faster, better. Deadlier. Desperate, Rion had gone to Harper, needing the one pure thing in his life to wash away the dirtiness, the guilt. But she'd taken one look at his face and the crimson stains and freaked, demanding he leave the gang. God, she'd been so innocent. No one just *left* the O'Bannon gang. And he couldn't abandon Killian and Sasha. Not even when she'd kissed him, and he'd taken it, for the first time tasting the sweetness that had been taunting him since high school.

So he'd pushed her away. The hands that had committed acts he was too ashamed to tell her about hadn't been worthy enough to touch her. What she'd wanted from him—a relationship—he couldn't give. What had he known of relationships? Quick fucks in a backseat or alley? Hell, he'd lost his virginity to a prostitute his father had bought and proudly gifted Rion with for his fifteenth birthday.

She'd deserved someone who could give her the white picket fence, the life in suburbia…safety. The gang life would have used her up, stolen the light from her eyes, replaced innocence with a world-weariness she should never wear.

That's what he could have offered her at the time.

And when she'd come to him and told him she'd accepted her boyfriend of six months' proposal, he hadn't stopped her. No matter how much those doe eyes had begged him to.

No matter how much it had killed him inside.

He turned at the soft click of his office door closing, deliberately schooling his features into a cold mask. Harper hovered on the top of the two steps that led to his office, her hand still wrapped around the doorknob. As if unsure whether to run or flee. He smothered a snort. Too late for that.

Sex. I need you for sex.

His cock thumped against his zipper as her admission slid through his mind, stroked down his chest, stomach, and fisted his dick. Much too late for that. She should've left when he'd given her the chance. Now she wasn't leaving without giving him an explanation. Mainly why didn't she go to her husband for sex. Still, no mistake.

She would be leaving.

"You wanted to talk privately," he said, leaning back against his desk and curling his fingers around the edge. That, or surrender to the urge to bury his hands into the thick mass of hair framing her face and covering the thrust of her breasts. "Don't have second thoughts now," he murmured, detesting the hoarseness creeping into his voice.

"I'm not having second thoughts," she objected, carefully descending the steps and pausing several feet away from him.

He waited for her to look at him, and when she finally did, he aimed a pointed stare at the fingers she twisted in front of her belly. A wince crossed her face. Lowering her hands to the sides of the black dress, which revealed slender legs that seemed much too long for a woman with her petite stature, she straightened her shoulders, her gaze unwavering. Still stubborn. Regardless of the names her parents had called him—or even what he'd said about himself—she'd defied them all to be his friend. When no one else had seen the good in him, she had, never failing to tell him he was better than the life he'd been born into.

"The photographs," she murmured, studying several of his, which were mounted and enlarged on his office walls. "They're yours. The ones downstairs, too."

"Yes." It was all he was willing to say on the subject. "Maybe you should reconsider this," he growled. "I think your husband would appreciate it."

She flinched, a spasm of pain twisting her face. "Terrance died," she whispered after several long seconds. "I'm a widow."

Fuck.

"I'm sorry, Harper." And he was. Yes, he hated that she'd given herself to another man, but he wouldn't wish the agony of losing a loved one on anyone. Least of all her. "How long ago?"

"Two years." She glanced away from him. "An aneurysm."

"I'm sorry, baby," he repeated. Her head jerked back, the same surprise cascading through him at his slip widening her eyes. *Shit*. He didn't use pet names, endearments. Ever. But this woman seemed capable of making him break his rules. "Yet that doesn't explain why you're here."

She lifted a shoulder, holding her hands out, palms up. "I already did. I—"

"Need me; I heard you. Sex," he murmured. A flush darkened her patrician cheekbones, those lush, carnal lips parting. His fingers itched with the urge to press a thumb to the plump curve, watch it indent under the pressure before he slid it forward and into her mouth, over her tongue. God, he wanted that. Which was why he couldn't have it. "What were you thinking? I lay you down on a bed? Or no, you probably want something more"—he twisted his lips into a smile—"exotic. Maybe my desk? Yeah, you want me to lay you down on the desk and, what? Flip your skirt up and get down to it? Sorry, baby. What I do isn't gentle, clean, or quick. You have no idea what I call sex, and you don't want to know. You're not *ready* to know."

She'd lifted her velvet gaze to him again. He'd expected anxiety, maybe even fear. But no. No fear. Arousal. Hot need glazed her eyes, darkening them to near black. Damn, he needed his camera. Needed to capture that look, immortalize it. That photo he would hang in his bedroom so when he fell asleep, it would be with her hunger for what he could give her in his mind, imprinting his dreams.

"That make you wet?" he murmured, a part of him knowing the answer. "Does the thought of me getting you messy and sweaty have your thighs squeezing?"

She stared at him, silent. Then…she nodded.

He narrowed his eyes at her. "Is it me? Is it the thought of my cock that has your pussy hot? Or would any do?"

"You," she whispered. But something flickered in her eyes. There and gone before he could decipher it. "I want you."

"Why?" he demanded. "Why me, and after this long?"

She crossed her arms, and the gesture reeked of defiance. "Once, you turned down what I offered you, even though you had no problem taking the same thing from other women. I want what you so willingly gave them."

"So you're slumming it now. Now you're looking for those quick screws in bathrooms and basements?"

"You said you don't do quick," she softly reminded him.

"But you're okay with slumming," he sneered.

Her eyes widened. "No, I didn't—"

"Forget it," he snapped, slashing a hand through the air as if he could cut off the conversation. What the hell was he doing? Not just taunting her and tormenting himself with the fact that she had lowered herself to come to him, but he tortured himself with what he couldn't have. With what wasn't his. Didn't matter that Terrance was gone; she still didn't belong with him. Didn't belong *here*, in Lick. She was too… untried. Again the word "innocent" tickled his mind. Yeah, she was too innocent for this place. For him.

"You don't know what you're asking for. What you *think* you want. How could you? What? Sex for you most likely consisted of years of missionary position with the lights out, nightgown pushed up around your waist." She emitted a helpless whimper, pressing her fingertips to her lips. Even imagining her and Terrance having such pathetic sex put a blow torch to his gut. "I'm close, aren't I?" He slowly pushed to his feet. "Come here."

Surprise flared in her dark eyes, but after a small hesitation, she moved toward him. He studied the subtle, but sexy, sway of her hips, and his fingers throbbed with the need to capture the swell of flesh between his palms and jerk her forward. Cradle and stroke his aching dick against her stomach. Instead he shifted to the side and jerked his chin.

"Go to the desk," he ordered, his fingers curling at his sides. She slid a questioning glance his way, but did as he demanded, coming to a halt in front of the piece of furniture. "Turn around and pull up your dress. And bend over."

Her shoulders stiffened, and he caught her low, sharp gasp. Her lips parted, her wide eyes searching his face. He didn't speak, just waited for her to push past him and run the hell out of his office and club. He'd warned her. She couldn't even obey a simple, relatively tame command. No way was she prepared…

Slowly, she pivoted on those ridiculously hot heels, presenting the slim line of her spine to him. Her fingers clutched the sides of her dress and inched the skirt high… higher…higher…

Fuck. Lust pummeled the air from his lungs. Black lace molded soft-looking, smooth flesh. Her ass. Goddamn, a work of erotic art. Moisture fled his mouth at his first look at the curves he'd fantasized about since he'd been a teenager. All the blood in his body rushed to his cock, pounding and demanding he thrust against the dark crease he could glimpse through the delicate material.

A lesson. This was a lesson.

The reminder did nothing to calm the hunger to touch, to shape, to fucking take.

"Bend over," he murmured, approaching her. "Palms flat on the desk, ass in the air." Easing to her side, he dragged a finger up the back of her thigh, and ruthlessly lassoed the shudder that wanted to work its way through his body at his first, sensual touch.

Harper didn't bother. He didn't miss the shiver that lightly shook her frame as she complied with his request.

"You hesitated. You think you can handle being here, handle fucking me when you pause with this." He trailed a caress up the inside of her thigh, teasing the edge of her panties, skirting the panel that covered her sex. "What are you going to do when I tell you to bend over, spread your legs…" He moved behind her, gently kicked her feet farther apart. "And don't move as I finger this sweet, little pussy in a room full of people?"

Without hesitation, he slipped beneath the strip of cloth shielding her from him and slid into hot, wet—so fucking *wet*—flesh. Smothering a groan, he stroked her slit, coating his finger in moisture he just knew would be sweet on his tongue. Sweet and addictive.

A lesson, damn it.

Firming his resolve, his determination, he palmed her waist, holding her steady as he circled her clit, strumming it. Her whimper reached his ears, and he tightened his grip, controlling the seductive, hungry roll of her hips. The nub at the top of her sex flexed and pulsed beneath his fingertip, and he growled as she widened her stance, silently begging for more. And he gave it to her; nothing could stop him from giving it to her. He rubbed her clit harder, polishing the bundle of nerves with a firmer stroke, pushing her. She bucked against his fingers, her fingers curling into the top of the desk.

Leaning over her arched back, he brushed her hair aside with his free hand. "You've probably never surrendered total control to a man," he growled in her ear. "Probably never sucked a man off, had him hold your head still while he shoots off down your throat. Never kneeled before him, wrists bound behind you, face to the sheets, ass in the air, pussy wet and open for him like you are now. I'd bet my left nut you don't know the pleasure/pain of having that same ass taken, fucked. Smuggled porn videos and YouTube clips can't prepare you for all that you're naively asking me to show you." He removed his hand from her panties, even as everything in him cursed him to hell and back. Gritting his teeth, he backed away from her, curling his drenched fingers into a fist as if he could capture the evidence of her desire in his skin. Keep it as a sensory memory. He forced himself to retreat another step from her shuddering form. "Go back home to your safe suburbs, baby."

Silence loomed between them like a dark specter, the only sound in the office her soft pants as she remained bent over the furniture. Lust pounded in his flesh, thickening it, sensitizing it so the press of his zipper was just about too much to bear. One touch. One squeeze. That's all it would take for him to explode, come so hard, it would damn near blind him.

Slowly, maybe as the realization that he wouldn't be finishing what he'd started dawned, she straightened, shock gradually replacing the lust stamped on her lovely features.

"You bastard," she whispered, jerking down her dress. Hiding herself from him.

He folded his arms across his chest. Arched an eyebrow.

"You're not ready for it. Not even almost."

"I want it," she insisted, pressing her palms to her belly, as if the request—the demand—had come straight from there. "Everything you described. I want it, Rion." Pause. "More. Give it to me."

Give it to me. Christ, she shouldn't ask that of someone like him—selfish, greedy, ruthless. He would take and take until she'd surrendered everything. And he craved everything. Her breathless cries, her shudders, her mouth, her breasts, her pussy, her ass. Her submission. He'd denied himself this before, but now he'd leave nothing untouched or hidden. And then he'd send her packing. Because she'd been his teacher in depending on someone, investing your heart and soul in someone, only to have them disappear. He wasn't up for another lesson. "Do you know what Lick is, Harper?" he demanded. "You've seen the public part. But we're not just some place you go to for a girls' night out, drinks, and dancing. Do you understand what goes on up here?" He waved a hand, indicating not just his office but the entire second floor of lofts.

"Yes," she breathed. "I've read things online. Rumors."

"I can promise whatever you've read doesn't begin to cover it." He chuckled, the low burst of laughter humorless. "And yet you're still standing here. Why?"

Her normally expressive features hardened for the briefest second, concealing her thoughts like a door suddenly slammed shut. "Because I want to."

The stiff, non-responsive reply pissed him off. She was hiding something. "Not good enough," he snapped. "This isn't a mommy porn fantasy. You'll be asked to do things—to allow another person to do things—that require trust."

"I trust you," she said, and he gritted his teeth. She couldn't even trust him with the truth behind her presence here.

"You don't know me," he bit out.

She frowned. "You would never hurt me."

"Of course not." He arched an eyebrow, allowing a slight smile. "I'd never cause you pain unless it heightened your pleasure. And only then with your full agreement." All her former uncertainty and vulnerability seemed to leave her as her gaze flared with heat. He sobered. "But that doesn't mean you couldn't end up in a situation you believe you're ready for, but aren't."

"How are you so certain I'm not ready? That I'm just a bored suburban housewife looking for a little slap and tickle?" Eyes narrowed, her voice shook with anger. "You have no idea what I need. How can you when I'm trying to figure it out myself?"

Her outburst vibrated in the air like a tossed gauntlet. One he had no intention of picking up.

"Which is exactly why you shouldn't be here," he said, his tone deliberately flat. Final. "My answer is no."

She rocked back, her lips parting in shock. But in the next instant, she steadied and squared her shoulders. "Fine. I'm not going to beg you. I'm through with that." What the hell was that supposed to mean? Had she begged someone else? Anger curled in his chest, a tight, burning knot. Who? "One thing I've learned in the last few years is life doesn't come to you; you have to grab it for yourself. And I'm tired of waiting, of depending on other people to decide what is right for me or what I need—deserve. *I* do that. I'm doing it. So if you won't help me, give me what I need, someone else will."

She turned, and a veil of crimson slammed down over his eyes.

"The hell you will," he snarled. Fuck that. *Fuck. That.* He shot across the floor and slammed a palm against the door. The barest of inches separated his chest from her back, his erection from the worship-worthy curve of her ass. He drew in a rough breath. Surrendered to the need to brush his lips over her hair. "Do you think you can threaten me?" he rasped.

"Don't try to force my hand, baby. I'm not the boy you knew."

"And I'm not the girl you knew," she shot back, turning to face him. She sank her teeth into her bottom lip, and he fought not to soothe the offended flesh…to slick his tongue over it. "If you don't do this for me, I'll find someone who will. Your club isn't the only one in Boston. I'm going to do this, Rion. Once I walk out of this club, you won't see me again."

"Just what do you plan on doing, Harper? Going home with any random motherfucker who promises to turn you out?"

"God, you're like a dog with a bone. You don't want me, but no one else can have me either?" She cocked her head to the side. "But that doesn't matter because it's not your business, is it?"

"You're playing a dangerous game, Harper," he warned.

"Only if I lose," she whispered.

They stared at one another, a high-noon showdown that neither backed down from. In her dark brown eyes, he spied determination. Resolution. *Damn it*. Bile churned in his gut and raced up the back of his throat at the thought of some bastard putting his hands on her creamy skin. Kissing her, screwing her. Another man wouldn't give a damn about her needs, about calming her fears and introducing her to the kind of sex she believed she wanted. No. Not going to happen.

Slowly, he dragged his hands down her arms, pausing to squeeze her wrists, then released her. He stepped back, placing distance between them. But not far. Close enough he could still inhale her sultry, strawberry-and-cream scent. Sweet, clean, mouth-watering. And soon he would have it. Anticipation, hot and thick, rolled through him.

"All right, Harper," he drawled. "You win. But I have one condition." He paused. Waited for her nod. "One night. I'll give you everything you came here looking for. I'll fuck you. Make you get on your knees for me. Make you come. Over and over again. On my face. My fingers. My dick. As often and as hard as I say. But only for a night."

Because no way in hell would he grant her another opportunity to rip him apart. This time, he would be the one to walk away.

Chapter Three

She'd won. Why did that sound so ominous?

Harper studied Rion, but his stoic expression—hooded gray eyes, unsmiling mouth, sharp lines of his face—revealed nothing. That sent another shiver tripping down her spine, but it didn't eclipse the excitement swirling in her chest and belly. The delicious, *unsatisfied* pulsing of the flesh between her legs. Or the relief.

After cajoling and browbeating herself into entering Lick tonight, could she have started over at another club? Approached a complete stranger and asked him—trusted him—to introduce her to the pleasure, the release, she needed? Let him touch her like Rion just had? She shuddered at the thought of having another man's finger sliding through her folds, torturing her clit. No. God no. The answer reverberated inside her like a struck gong.

And, almost as important, was his stipulation. One night. Fine. She hadn't come here for more than sex. Open herself up to the agony of loss and disappointments? No, thank you. On that condition, they were in complete agreement. Besides, it lined up with what she remembered about him, too. As he'd once told her, he didn't do relationships.

Yet, he was her private shame… No. Not Rion. Her lust for him. Her desire to have him stare at her with that hypnotic, steely gaze as he broke her with pleasure. To see his big body shudder over hers…feel him stretch and fill her… Even when she'd married another man.

Maybe her coming here, to him, had more to do with moving on with her life. Maybe it was an exorcism of sorts. Finally being with him—finally discovering for herself what being on the receiving end of his control, passion, and pleasure was like—would free her of *him*.

"What are your hard limits?" His question jerked her from the past, from herself.

She blinked. "I'm sorry?"

"Your hard limits," he repeated, his piercing scrutiny unsettling. As if he could peer into her thoughts and expose them one by one. "Since we only have a few hours, I need to know what you absolutely refuse to do, and what you're willing to explore."

Slowly, like a sleek, big cat, he circled her. Stalked her. As if he contemplated how to take her down. How to just take her.

"Harper?" he purred against her ear. Not one part of his body touched her, yet she felt surrounded by him. His heat, his wood, earth, and skin scent. And sex. He carried the fragrance of uninhibited, wild, raw sex in his skin.

"I hadn't thought…"

"Yeah, you have." Gentle but firm fingers pinched her chin and tipped her head to the side, tilting it up. His dark, knowing gaze captured hers as effectively as his hand clasped her face. "Don't lie to me. Whatever you tell me here, whatever we do—you're safe. There's no shame, no guilt in anything we do or say. I promise not to use anything against you, not to hurt you. And in exchange, you give me honesty. We clear?"

She nodded. Honesty, talking—they weren't her strong suits. For her, honesty, at least about her feelings, had been sacrificed for compromise. Talking had been martyred for not rocking the boat. But to have this—to have him for this night—she would try. Trusting him would begin before she removed one article of clothing, before one kiss or touch. For her, it was the biggest risk.

"Good," he murmured, removing his grip. "Now, answer my question."

Closing her eyes, she inhaled, and took the plunge. "No asphyxiation."

"What about this?" He slid a hand around her collar bone, and she shuddered at the intimate contact. Though he was a businessman, calluses toughened his palm, and they abraded her skin, a direct contrast to the softness of the caress. "Easy," he soothed, the low timbre of his voice another layer of touch. Slowly, he eased his hand up until his fingers and thumb encircled her throat and applied the lightest of pressure. He didn't squeeze, didn't shut off her air supply. But the warm, sensual weight of him there bottomed out her belly, had her clenching her thighs against the thrilling pulse there, against the rush of liquid heat. An image of them together, his hand around her neck, drawing her up and back as he fucked her from behind shimmered across the back of her eyelids. Her breath hitched in her throat, and she whimpered. The hold was dominant, controlling, but not frightening.

"No?" he asked.

"Yes," she breathed. Slicked the tip of her tongue over her bottom lip. "I—this is okay."

She felt his nod as he released her. "What else?"

"I don't want to be gagged or masked." They struck too close to home; she'd endured both in her marriage, figuratively, anyway. She wanted to be free of them.

Rion stilled behind her as if he wanted to question, but instead he rubbed his cheek against her hair. "Blindfold?"

She shrugged. "I'm not against it. I…" She swallowed—*courage*—and confessed before she could surrender to the urge to stifle it. "I want to watch."

Even though he'd promised her he wouldn't use anything she'd shared against her, she still waited, bracing herself for the ridicule, the shaming. Unbidden, Terrance's voice lashed out at her like a ghost from beyond the grave. *Do you want me to treat you like a slut on the street? You're a wife, not a whore. Act like it.*

But it didn't come. And the relief almost buckled her knees.

"Anything else?" he pressed.

"I don't know," she admitted, and huffed, disgust at herself heavy in the sound. "God, you must think I'm an idiot. Or worse. A *Fifty Shades* wannabe."

"I've thought many things about you over the years and tonight. Idiot isn't one of them." His fingers on her hip tightened briefly. "You said you like to watch." When she nodded, he splayed his big hand across her belly, his thumb grazing the underside of her breast. A tease of a touch. Nowhere near enough. "Okay. Do you like a little pain, Harper? Enough to sharpen the pleasure? Paddling. Spanking your clit. Can I spread you wide, tie you down?"

"Yes," she said on a gust of breath. *Oh God, yes*.

"I can have your pussy, but what about your ass? Ever let a man take you there, Harper?"

She shook her head, lust stealing her ability to speak. "No. Never." She swayed, her ass brushing against his erection. Damn. He was hard…big. Her sex spasmed, milking emptiness. It *hurt*. "I-I don't know. Maybe."

"We'll go slow," he promised. "If something makes you uncomfortable, tell me, and we'll stop, okay?" She nodded, and he grazed his lips over her ear. Technically their first kiss. "Give me a word, Harper. We won't do anything hardcore, but I still need a safe word from you. If you say it, I stop, no going back. It ends."

His assurance comforted her. This might have been a fool's errand—running headlong into a situation she really couldn't comprehend with her limited knowledge. But with Rion guiding her, she was safe, protected. And damn it, she wanted it. Needed it. Whatever he would show her tonight, expose her to... She. *Needed*. It.

"Rosebud." From *Citizen Kane*. The first movie they'd watched together. Rion's favorite, starring his idol, Orson Welles.

Silence followed her murmur, and Rion stiffened. Tension seemed to vibrate from him, and she curled her fingers into a fist. *Stupid*. She shouldn't have introduced sentimentality into this. She should have—

"Fine." He slid his hands down her arms, covered her clenched fingers. Slowly unfurled them and enfolded them in his. "Welcome to my world, Harper."

Chapter Four

What are you doing?

The question ricocheted off the walls of Rion's skull as he led Harper from his office and into the dark hallway. His conscience tried to poke the *What the hell* stick at him, but the lust beating at him like a fist and the delicate but heavy weight of her hand in his overrode any pricks of latent morality. The fact he was corrupting the one person he'd once prayed would remain innocent and pure didn't elude him. He'd been everything her parents had called him—trouble, no good, a gangbanger—and he'd tried to stay away from her. But when Harper would have none of that, he'd protected her instead. And now, years later, he was the one escorting her into a world that she shouldn't even know existed.

The devil would have his name on a special VIP list for this.

"Oh my God, Rion, it's beautiful." She halted behind him, tugging her hand free. He turned as she lifted a hand to the mural on the wall. Because of the dim lighting provided only by mounted sconces, many people didn't spot the deep reds, blues, and purples of the art surrounding them. But he hadn't added the paintings for them—they were for him. Still, like the photography, Harper had noticed. Because she knew him like no other person, aside from Sasha and Killian.

He stepped back and slipped his hands in his pants pockets, granting her the time to study the art. Her delighted gasps and murmurs sent satisfaction surging through him.

"It's *The Masque of the Red Death*." She sighed, tracing the tall grandfather clock with its hands forever frozen at midnight with her fingertips. She moved on to the masked revelers in their ornate costumes, the grand ballroom with a delicate but hypnotizing chandelier, and the mysterious robed figure. The short story by Edgar Allan Poe, with its symbolism and darkness, had been one of their favorites. "You…" She glanced at him over her shoulder, wonder lacing her voice.

"I commissioned it." Building the club had been a joint effort, but his friends had left the decor to Rion. He hadn't been stingy with money or the thought put into each aspect of the design. And he would also be a liar if he claimed Harper hadn't entered his mind when he'd detailed what he wanted in The Loft. After he'd stepped in when two asshole jocks had her pinned against the lockers, knocking textbooks out of her hands and squeezing her ass on the sly, she'd befriended him. Even when he'd initially tried to ice her out. Harper had been stubborn in her quiet way. So he'd relented. Knowing he could never bring her home to his shitty apartment where his father laid out his guns like her mother probably displayed *Better Homes and Gardens* magazines. Knowing he could never walk her down the streets of his neighborhood because to the men loitering on those corners and in the doorways, she would be seen as a thing they could use, abuse, or kill to get to Rion. And yet, he'd still hoarded her friendship.

And she'd introduced him to the classics such as Edgar Allan Poe, Nathaniel Hawthorne, H.P. Lovecraft, and movies like *Citizen Kane, Journey into Fear*, and *Othello*. She'd opened up a new, vibrant, beautiful world that had been shut off to him before. If not for the unforgiving, ruthless existence he'd been born into where the son of a mob hitman didn't waste time on "sissy shit," he might've been a cinematographer, combining his love of movies and photography. Through sheer doggedness, and Harper's unflagging belief in him, he'd suffered his father's disdain and occasional beatings and refused to give up on dreams of something better. This—the club, his friends by his side, his freedom, and his photography—was his better.

"I based the idea of The Loft on the story," he revealed.

"The Loft?" She turned, an eyebrow arched.

"This upper level"—he waved his hand—"is The Loft. It's a part of Lick but separate from downstairs. To gain entrance here, a person has to go through an intense application process. We interview applicants as well as conduct a background investigation. That might seem overboard, but all things considered, it's not just prudent but necessary."

"All things considered?" she repeated, slower, and maybe just a bit wary.

Good.

"Harper, do you know what an aphrodisiac club is?" He stalked closer to her, not stopping until his chest was a breath away from grazing hers. Though lust simmered in his gut, he didn't touch her. The conscience he'd believed drowned out, waved one last desperate arm, offering her another opportunity to back away from this path she seemed determined to tread. "It's not a BDSM club. Or rather not just a BDSM club. We offer more than that. Whatever a person finds sexually exciting aside from demeaning or unsanitary fetishes and illegal acts, we offer. It's not just about the kink—although there's plenty of that—it's also about the fantasy. Behind each door"—he nodded at the multi-colored doors on either side of the hall—"is a room for a particular desire. If you want to be spanked, tied down, watched, or just somewhere to express yourself, Lick is a safe place to do so."

"I know what you're trying to do," she breathed. "You're trying to warn me away again. But that doesn't scare me. It sounds…beautiful." She sighed, and the whisper of sound seemed almost wistful, envious. "Freeing," she added.

Unable to help himself, he cupped her jaw and rubbed his thumb across her lush bottom lip. "Freeing? That's an odd choice of word. Have you been in prison until now, Harper?" What had that asshole she was married to done to her?

"All of us are in some way or another, right?" She deflected the question, but he didn't miss the forced nonchalance in her voice. He'd allow it…for now. But at some point tonight, she would give him the answer. "Will you show me now?"

He leveled one last, long look at her, and she met his stare. Neither moved except for his deliberately firm caress over her mouth. Finally, he dropped his hand and shifted backward. Once more, he enclosed her fingers in his and headed deeper into the world he and his friends had created.

Walls had been torn down and added in the converted space, fashioning rooms and large play spaces. As they neared the end of the corridor, he stopped in front of a light blue door. He opened it and strode inside, bringing Harper with him. Easing to the side and behind her, he allowed her to soak in the scene before her. Her sharp gasp reached his ears, and she stiffened, her fingers locking his in a vise grip.

She'd stated she wanted to watch. In this room, that need was not only indulged but encouraged.

Several leather couches of varying lengths, large armchairs, and long, wood tables dotted the large room. Dim light from three sconces deepened the shadows in the black-painted room. On the wall nearest them, a bartender served drinks to the twenty or so people occupying the area. The ages of the men and women ran the gamut from early twenties to early sixties, and they wore tuxedoes, expensive dresses, jeans, and slinky mini-dresses that barely covered their asses. Several lounged on the couches, drinks in hand. Some men had women perched on their laps, hands casually fondling breasts or sliding between parted, bare legs. Others leaned against the walls or crowded into the corners, their grunts and low cries peppering the air.

But none of them were the focal point of the room.

The naked couple behind the glass wall held that honor.

The couple, a well-built man, his dark hair cut close to his head, and a slim, blonde woman with breasts too buoyant to be real, stretched out on a wrought-iron bed that wouldn't have been out of place in a country bed and breakfast. The bed rested on a raised platform and was turned sideways so the audience had an unhindered view. The large, white pillows and eyelet blankets added a sweetness to the sin taking place on top of them.

Looming over his woman, the man drew a berry-colored nipple into his mouth, sucking so hard on the tip, she cried out, her back arching. A large hand slid down her flat stomach and disappeared between her legs, stroking bare flesh, already glistening with moisture. Without releasing her nipple, he spread her thighs wider, pressing them flat to the bed so their audience had a perfect, erotic view of his thick fingers sliding through her flushed, pink lips and dipping into her pussy. Even through the glass partition, her cry of pleasure reached them.

A shudder rippled through Harper, and he gently shook his hand free from hers and placed both of his on her hips, steadying her.

"R-Rion," she stammered, inching backward. He pressed his chest to her back, notched his cock against the high rise of her ass and the dip in her spine. Unlike before, he didn't try to hide her effect on him. He wanted her to feel what she did to him. What she would take in her mouth and pussy before the night was over. She released a small whimper but didn't move. Didn't flee the room. That sign of need, of *trust*, made his flesh harden more until he damn near resembled stone.

"This is the voyeur room," he murmured in her ear. "Look around, Harper. All these people have the same desire as you. To watch others fuck. They love it; they get off on it. Just like you." He shifted her toward the back of the room and, pressing his spine to the wall, widened his legs and drew her between them. Her gaze was riveted to the sensual scene being played out in front of them. Her chest rose and fell on rapid breaths, her fingers twisting in front of her. He covered her hands with one of his own, halting the nervous fidgeting.

In the adjoining room, the man eased to the floor and knelt between his woman's legs. As if presenting a beautiful, priceless treasure, he spread her legs wide, allowing them to see her swollen, wet folds. Taking pride in her restless grinding of hips, arching back, and needy plucking at her own nipples, he trailed his lips up one calf and down a toned, pale thigh, toward her pussy. In front of him, tension entered Harper's frame, and she stilled. And when the man bypassed the woman's sex, instead repeating his caress on her other leg, Harper's frustrated sigh echoed the other woman's growl. Again, that tension crept back into her frame when the man neared his partner's drenched flesh. This time, his tongue licked a slow path up her slit, flicking the clit. Several long, lust-filled groans filled the room. Including one from Harper.

Tearing his gaze from the scene, Rion dropped it to her face, needing to witness the pleasure that vibrated against his chest.

Fuck. The muted lighting couldn't hide the wide eyes darkened by surprise and pleasure or her parted lips. Couldn't conceal the flush painting her high, sculpted cheekbones or slashing across the skin her scooped, modest neckline revealed. Lust looked gorgeous on her. She was meant to wear it.

Harper leaned against him as if her legs could no longer bear her weight. A peek back at the glass showed the man working the woman over with long, hungry strokes, teasing laps, and greedy sucks. Slowly, Rion spread his fingers wide over Harper's belly. God, she was so fucking tiny. Each hand spanned her stomach, throwing in sharp relief how much he dwarfed her. An image of them in bed taunted him. He would cover her completely, dominate her. Would her petite body be able to take the rough, dirty sex he liked? Could she, so delicate and small, take all of his dick inside her undoubtedly tight and equally small pussy? Sweat dampened his palms and the base of his spine at the thought. He'd only caressed the damp folds, and inching himself inside her would be torture and pleasure. Both guaranteed to kill him.

But, sweet fuck, what a way to go.

Slowly, he slid his hands up her torso and cupped her breasts. She jerked hard in his hold, releasing a startled cry.

"Shh," he soothed, nuzzling her ear. He placed a soft kiss behind her ear, and she twitched again. Noting that spot, he whispered, "Easy, baby."

This time, he didn't regret the endearment. Not here, in the dark, with sex riding the air like a perfume. Like he'd assured her, everything was allowed. No regrets. No shame. What he couldn't utter if they'd met on the street or even downstairs, he could here. Squeezing her flesh, he hummed, pleasure a hot, tight knot in his gut. Even with the dress in the way, she filled his hands. Not overflowing like the woman writhing on the bed, but natural, enough. Perfect.

He stared down over her shoulder, stared at his hands cradling her tits, shaping them, molding them. Part of him couldn't believe he was finally—*finally*—touching Harper. That same part held its breath, waiting for him to wake up from another wet dream, his dick in his hand. But no. She was real. Harper, his Harper—because for the next few hours before he let her go, she belonged to him—stood in front of him, her ass wedged against his cock, her fingers locked around his wrists, her nipples at rigid attention under his thumbs.

Her head dropped on his shoulder, but her eyes remained on the couple where the man tongue-fucked his woman. She'd curled her hands behind her knees, trapping her thighs to her chest, granting her lover unhindered access to her pussy. Yeah, it was hot. But not as arousing as the slick of Harper's tongue over her lips. Or the tiny sounds she emitted as Rion pinched her nipples.

Shaking her hands loose, he skimmed his down her arms and drew them over her head and behind his neck. He squeezed her fingers, ensuring she understood not to move, then gathered the heavy silk of her hair and flipped the dark strands over her shoulder. The tab of her dress called to him, and he answered, tugging the zipper down. The material parted, exposing inch after inch of smooth, dusky skin. She carried the evidence of her Italian heritage in the olive and porcelain tone. Made a man hungry and thirsty at the same time.

For a moment, he just stared at the slice of skin, once more reverting to that young man who had been offered the chance to touch, but with blood on his hands, hadn't been clean or worthy enough to take. The one who had stood there, stoic and raging inside when she'd gutted him by choosing to marry someone with her parents' stamp of approval.

But that youth no longer existed. The man who would take her over and over again tonight, satiating the craving that had dogged him for years, did. And he would do just that before walking away and never looking back.

Grim satisfaction prowled through him as he unhooked

her bra strap and slid his hands inside the dress, smoothing his palms over her skin. *Hell yes*. He clenched his teeth, trapping the deep groan that rose in his chest. So soft. Exactly as he remembered. He almost snatched his hands from her, worried they would bruise her. Only her earlier assurance that she could take whatever he dealt her kept him from reacting... That, and the arousal blasting his insides like a blowtorch.

Pressing his temple to hers, he once again cupped her, slipping under her loosened bra. Flesh to flesh. Skin to skin. She jolted, arching into palms, fingernails digging into his nape. Relishing the bite of pain, he kneaded her breasts and pinched her nipples into tight, hard tips. Dipping his head, he trailed his lips up the elegant column of her neck and continued to torment them both. God, he wanted to jerk the dress down to her waist, bare her to his eyes and mouth. Instead he tugged on the peaks, rolling and flicking them. Harper twisted and writhed under his touch, her whimpers and low moans like a sensual symphony. She was his instrument to pluck, to play.

Once more, he wished for his camera. Fuck, what he wouldn't give to photograph her right now. To capture the sweet undulations of her petite body and the passion that tore gasps from her parted lips and clouded her beautiful eyes.

Eyes that were closed.

"Open your eyes," he ordered, giving her breasts one last squeeze before removing his hands from her dress and gripping her hips. "Look at them."

Her lashes fluttered, her head rising off his shoulder. Together, they watched the man deliver another long lick to his lover's folds, pausing to tease her clit with the tip of his tongue. Then he rose and crawled over her, his muscled form crouched over her much slimmer one. He shifted her body, so their audience had the perfect view of his back, ass...and her flushed, shining pussy.

"Rion," she whispered.

Rion tightened his hold on her, guiding her to an armchair tucked in the deeper shadows a couple of feet away. Instead of seating her on the cushion, he led her behind the chair, and tangling her fingers with his, curled them over the back. She twisted, glancing at him over her shoulder, but he grasped her chin and gently, but firmly, turned her forward again. With the tip of his shoe, he nudged her feet wider, and with a palm to her lower back, silently ordered her to lean forward.

"Watch," he murmured, lowering his hands to the hem of her dress. He fisted the material, drawing the skirt up her slim legs, once more baring her inch by slow inch. She trembled, the quivers like aftershocks coursing through her and vibrating against him. With a low growl, he brushed his lips down her spine, and the shivers intensified. He straightened, fierce pleasure and satisfaction that he could make her shake and shudder pulsed inside him like a heartbeat. Determined to earn more, he finished bunching her dress around her hips, exposing her to his hungry stare.

Sin and innocence wrapped in black lace. Not the thongs most women of his acquaintance wore, but delicate lace cut high at her smooth thighs, again teasing him with glimpses of flesh underneath. One hand holding her skirt in place, he smoothed the other over one ass cheek, cupping it, squeezing it. *Yeah, I'm touching her*. That damn awe again. He trailed his fingers down the crease, hiding the tiny hole he wanted to caress, lick, and fuck…

She jerked. "Rion," she rasped his name and reached back and cuffed his wrist. The restraint was either in objection to him baring her from the waist down or to the illicit stroke. "I'm not—" she stammered.

"You okay, baby?" he rasped, pausing. No one paid them attention, but he had to make sure she was comfortable, that she felt only pleasure, not embarrassment or, worse, shame. "You good with this?"

"Yes," she breathed. After a moment, she returned her hand to the back of the chair. "Yes."

"Good," he praised, pressing his chest to her back, covering her. His thighs brushed the insides of hers, preventing her from closing her legs. Rocking his hips forward, he stroked his dick against her ass like he'd wanted to do earlier. He nipped her earlobe in both praise and punishment at the pleasure she gave him. "Look at how wet she is. She's soaked. But not just for him. Because she knows all these eyes are on her. Because *your* eyes are on her." He flattened a palm to her belly and slid the other one down and over her hip. She sucked in a breath. "You're giving her pleasure just by watching, by getting hot and drenched. And you are wet, aren't you, Harper?" He teased the band of her panties, slipping just his fingertips underneath. Soft, springy hair grazed his skin, and he ground his dick harder against her. Gritting his teeth, he growled, "Harper? Answer me."

"Yes." The word exploded from between her lips on a gasp. Tilting her head back, she rocked her ass up and down, rubbing over his dick, and dragging a groan out of him. "God, I am. Please, Rion. Just…"

He plunged two fingers inside her at the same time the man on the other side of the glass buried himself inside his lover's pussy. A low, keening wail erupted from her, drowning out his hoarse "fuuuuuck."

Slick, muscular walls. Hot like a furnace. Liquid heat that, by all rights, should be scalding him. She spasmed around his fingers, quivering as her flesh accustomed itself to the invasion. Goddamn, she was small. Tight. Perfect.

His cock throbbed as if jealous, and hell, it should be. Pushing inside her would be hell…and the only glimpse of heaven he would ever be granted.

Withdrawing his fingers, he glided them through her slit, and over her engorged little clit. Harper bucked against his hand, wild sounds spilling out of her. Jesus, she was hot. Just one thrust and caress and, that fast, she was on the verge of coming undone. With a snarl, he grasped her chin, tilted it down, forcing her attention on the fucking in front of them.

The man pounded into his woman, his dick disappearing in her thrust after thrust. The slap of flesh filled the room even through the glass. And the sighs and grunts from the others in the room, as well as from the woman in his arms, steadily rose.

"That's what I'm going to do to you," he growled, wrapping his arm around her waist, holding her still as he rocketed his fingers back into her sex. Like a good girl, she didn't move her hands from the chair, but she writhed against him, voluntarily spreading her legs wider so he could have more of her. Setting up a fast, steady pace, he pumped into her, lust like a clawing beast digging at his gut every time her lush walls squeezed him. "I'm going to fuck you into the bed. Hard. Deep. Imagine this"—he twisted his wrist, corkscrewing his fingers and ripping a cry free of her—"is my dick, riding you, screwing you, branding this pretty, tight as hell pussy. You're going to scream for me, baby. Again." He thrust into her. "And again." Thrust. "And again."

He dipped his other hand between her thighs and circled the taut bud at the top of her thighs, torturing the engorged bundle of nerves with firm strokes. His fist bumped the soft skin of her inner thighs as he slammed his fingers into her, pushing her closer and closer to orgasm.

"Come, baby," he whispered, rubbing her clit as he plunged hard and high within her sex. "Come with her. Give it to me and her."

She came, strangling his fingers in a vise-like grip. She shook with the force of it, and he didn't let up on his thrusts or caresses to her clit until every last shudder quieted. Behind the partition, the woman's cries rebounded off the glass, her legs splayed wide as her man rode her through the release.

Harper whimpered with her as she slumped back against him, her chest rising and falling on her still harsh breaths.

Slowly, he eased his fingers from inside her, reluctant to leave. Still feeling the death-grip of her pussy, he slid them into his mouth, humming as the first taste of her exotic flavor exploded across his senses. Damn. Sweet. Tangy. Fucking addicting. He sucked her cream clean. And it only whetted his appetite for more.

Lust beat inside him. He needed to be inside her. Her mouth, her pussy, her ass—just *inside*. But this—this dip into voyeurism—had been for her…for her to let go. To realize she could. Reluctant pride surged within.

Tangling his fingers in her hair, he gathered it to the side and pressed a kiss to her neck, murmuring her name. She started, ducking her head, the movement quick. And it smacked of guilt. Lifting his gaze, he followed the line of direction where hers had been before he'd surprised her. It didn't take long to discover what had held her fascination.

Across the room, a woman with enough curves to shame Botticelli's Venus lay sprawled over the arm of one of the couches. And most of those curves were on full display. But he'd bet his left nut it wasn't her bared tits that had snared Harper's attention. Two men bent over the woman. One cradled a breast in his hand, sucking hard on the nipple, his fingers toying with the other. And the second man knelt between her spread thighs, his face buried in her pussy. Absolute carnal ecstasy suffused her face, twisting it into a mask of lust and arousal.

Is it the thought of my cock that has your pussy hot? Or would any do? The question he'd asked Harper in his office ghosted across his mind. As did the flicker of emotion in her eyes that he couldn't identify…then. Now he understood. Lust. Furtive and quickly hidden, but it'd been lust he'd glimpsed. Yeah, Harper wanted him—the force of her orgasm and his drenched fingers was proof of that. But she wanted *more*.

An image wavered and solidified in his head, and his gut tightened with need. Harper, splayed out on the couch, her face hard with pleasure as Rion ate her pussy while another man played with those pretty breasts.

Need, greedy and hot, surged through him.

"Do you want that, Harper?" Her head jerked up, and he studied her face. Caught the surprise and shame that flashed across her expression before she concealed it. He hated that guilt. Had seen it one too many times tonight. She, with her beauty, her passion, had nothing to be ashamed about. To feel dirty about. She parted her lips, but he waylaid her reply. "Honesty, baby," he reminded her.

"I…" She inhaled, slicked the tip of her tongue over her lips. With another quick peek at the trio, she shrugged a shoulder. "I don't know."

She knew. Was just afraid to voice the fantasy.

"Okay," he said, allowing her the lie…for now. "Are you ready?"

He didn't wait for her reply but tugged her skirt down, for now concealing what he considered his, even if only for the next few hours. Without bothering to zip her dress, he extended his hand to her, and once her smaller one pressed to his, he led her out of the room. As if attuned to some internal clock, he could feel the minutes ticking away. Soon his time with her would come to an end. But not before he made every second count.

Made every one of them a memory.

Chapter Five

"In here."

Harper walked past Rion and entered another room, noting the green door. Green. The color of youth, rebirth. Maybe that should've been the paint on the first room. Because damn, she'd been reborn in there. She'd discovered that all her life she'd been living in hues of gray, her world muted, placid. But now...now those blinders had been ripped away, and the colors were so vibrant, technicolor, alive, that it almost hurt. In that room, with the couple performing for them — no, not performing, because there had been no artifice between them. In that room, with the couple fucking for their pleasure, Rion had shattered her.

And the fear that had been missing when he'd warned her about what to expect, about what he planned to do to her, rushed in like a flood, crashing against her.

Because she didn't know if she would ever be able to pick up all those pieces she'd splintered into and reshape herself into something recognizable.

Still, if it was just the fear, she could recover quickly. Or at least fake it until the unsettling sense of foreboding dissipated. But the shame dogging fear's heels like a yipping dog refused to be silenced. Guilt's sibilant hiss filled her ears as it wound an oily, thick path through her veins, coating her heart.

"Are those second thoughts making a belated appearance?" Rion stood in front of her, and she focused her attention on the wide expanse of his chest, unable to meet his eyes.

"No."

"You were always a horrible liar," he mocked, shifting closer until she breathed in his dark, delicious scent. "Look at me, Harper."

Though soft, the tone brooked no argument or resistance. And she obeyed without hesitation. But this wasn't the resented acquiescence she'd given Terrance. With Rion, she *wanted* to surrender, trusting that her safety, her needs, her pleasure was first and foremost for him. She could entrust her body into his care without worry.

It was her heart that she couldn't risk.

It had been broken too many times and even now was held together by emotional duct tape.

He cocked his head to the side, studied her. "What was our agreement earlier? I don't use anything we do against you, and you give me what in return?"

"Honesty," she murmured.

"You haven't held up your end of the bargain, and I've let it go. But not now. What's wrong? This doesn't go any further until you tell me what you're thinking."

The urge to utter "rosebud," her safe word, rose within her, hovered on her tongue. She hadn't used it when he'd hiked her dress up in a room full of people and finger-fucked her. Yet, she was willing to say it because he pushed her to expose secrets she'd never intended for him to discover. Humiliation strangled her.

Coward.

Her own insult beat at her. She'd come to Lick to jumpstart her life, to find the woman who had dreamed of one day owning a book store and café, who had defied her parents to befriend a boy who moved in the dangerous, murky world of the mob. Uncover the woman she was meant to be. She hadn't backed down or given up when Rion had first rejected her. But now, at the thought of stripping free of her heart rather than her clothes, she was ready to turn tail and run.

Closing her eyes, she reached for the courage of that woman. "That—what we just did—it was...dirty."

"Yeah, it was."

Shocked, she met his hooded gaze.

"What?" he pressed. "It was dirty, hot, and good as hell. And you enjoyed every minute of it."

She shook her head, fighting the guilt, frustration, and burning arousal twisting inside her. His eyes narrowed.

"Are you going to try and claim you didn't love it?"

"No." Again she shook her head. "No, I did. I've never—" *Come like that before.* She bit the telltale admission off. "Just because I-I liked it doesn't make me a slut."

He recoiled, his head jerking back as if slapped by a phantom palm. Pinching the bridge of her nose, she sighed. God, she was mucking this explanation up. With a low growl, Rion crowded her, his chest and thighs pressed to hers. Fury had chased away the surprise, and it darkened his eyes, firmed the sensual curves of his lips into a flat, grim line.

"Hell no, it doesn't make you a slut. Who said it did?" Before she could reply, he slowly nodded, his lips twisting into a hard smile. "No, let me guess. Terrance. What happened? You asked for something more than missionary?"

Jesus. Embarrassment crawled over her, prickling her skin. Crossing her arms, she rubbed them, cringing inside from his question.

"Harper." That tone again. The one that demanded her honesty. Her truth. No matter how humiliating it was.

"I wanted to use…toys in bed. But that offended him, because it was basically saying he wasn't satisfying me. Then I asked him if we could watch…" She paused, squeezed her arms tighter. "…Movies together. If we could have sex while they were on. I thought it would be sexy. But he told me I wasn't a whore. That only whores wanted what I did." A dangerous, dark rumble of sound emanated from Rion, but she continued. "One Friday, he'd left home for his monthly poker game with friends. He usually stayed out until very late, so I put in a movie I'd secretly bought. In the middle of it, he returned home early and caught me. He…" She shifted her attention to the far wall over Rion's shoulder. "He lost it. Trashed the DVD player. Called me a slut and more horrible names. Said I was dirty. After that, I never asked him for anything more. Not even…"

Not even after she became pregnant, and he stopped having sex with her, treating her like some untouchable Madonna instead of a woman. She bit her lip, trapping the words in. That particular secret—her pregnancy, Carlie—she wasn't ready to share. Never would be.

"Not even, what?" Rion pushed, of course catching her reluctance to continue.

"Not even when I felt invisible as a woman. Unattractive. Undesirable. For so long, I've been a wife"—*a mother*—"a silent partner, a title rather than a person. For once, I just want to be desired, to be needed. To be…"

"Free," he supplied, his quiet tone a stark contradiction to hers.

She nodded, dropping her arms. "Free," she repeated just as softly, surprised he'd remembered her earlier admission in his office.

"Why did you marry him?"

Because you didn't stop me. She bit back the accusation. "We'd dated for a while," she began, hesitant. Careful not to admit too much. Like, she'd started seeing Terrance after Rion had rejected her. She'd accepted that first date with Terrance out of her desperation to overcome her insane and fruitless fascination with Rion. "So when he asked, I said yes." She shrugged. "Like you pointed out then, Terrance was a good man. He had a great job with his father at their accounting firm. I'd just graduated from college. And I…was ready to start my life."

Had she been in all-consuming insta-love and lust with Terrance like she'd been with Rion from the moment he'd warned those asshole bullies that he'd fuck them up if they came near her again? No. But she had loved and respected Terrance. And they'd shared common values and goals in life. Her parents had based their thirty-year marriage on the same foundation.

Besides, she'd wasted years wanting Rion. After he'd told her he didn't do relationships, refused to leave the life that would one day steal his, and had distanced himself from her, she'd had to move on as best as she could.

"But it wasn't what you wanted," he stated, tone flat.

"We weren't married long, but…no. I found out too late that Terrance wanted a homemaker, not a career woman as a wife, so I never used my business degree, thinking I could wear him down eventually. Then…" She shut down the thought of their baby with a teeth-jarring slam. "After a while, I just wanted peace and not to live in strife, so I went along. I mean, plans change all the time. But now, I know that peace at any cost isn't peace at all."

"Is that the reason behind your hard limits? No gags or masks?"

Once more, he surprised her. But then again, he was the most intuitive person she'd ever known, always watching people with that steady, piercing gray stare. At some point, he'd even seen past her we're-just-friends facade and guessed how much she craved him.

"Yes," she murmured. "I spent most of my marriage silent and wearing one figurative mask or another. I couldn't stand that here, between us."

He slipped a hand around her neck, cupping the nape in his big palm. She shivered under his masculine, dominant hold. He'd bared her in a room full of people, touched her, whispered dirty things to her, had made her come on his fingers, and yet, she'd never felt more sexy, wanted, and protected.

"Harper, wanting sex that doesn't fit into a narrow mold doesn't make you depraved or sinful or any of those other stupid labels people with sexual hang-ups try to tack onto others. You are a gorgeous, sensual woman who isn't afraid to explore her body or indulge in pleasure not just for herself, but her partner. You are giving and unselfish, and I damn near came from just watching you in that room. You're rare, and your curiosity, your passion deserves to be encouraged and cherished, not shamed. Terrance was wrong for making you feel like you were immoral. He was intimidated by you, by your needs and instead of being a considerate, selfless lover, he tried to make you feel guilty. It's probably a serious breach in etiquette to speak ill of the dead, but he had a gift, and he's a fucking fool for not appreciating it."

She sucked in a breath. No one had ever spoken to her like that. Her heart slammed against her rib cage. But beneath the clamor crept hope of maybe, just maybe, someone saw the real her—the flawed, stubborn her who fantasized about being corrupted…dirtied.

And even more, he accepted her.

"Thank you," she whispered.

"You want to thank me," he said, stroking a hand up her

thigh and cupping her, the heel of his palm pressing against her clit. She gasped, heat flooding to her sex, bringing a now familiar ache with it. "Then let me taste what my fingers have already touched."

Lust stole her ability to speak. Not that she would've said no. And maybe he'd guessed her answer because he released her neck and slid that hand under her dress as well. He hooked his fingers in the band of her panties and slid them down her legs. Then stepped back, his stormy scrutiny like a brand.

"Undress for me," he ordered.

A protest leaped to her lips. Him stripping her was one thing; he had the control. He was doing it *to* her. But if she removed her clothes, she would be laying herself bare. In more ways than one. Baring not just her skin but her insecurities and vulnerability. She was a far cry from the women who strutted around downstairs with their tight, barely clothed, model-thin bodies. The women he was probably used to fucking.

What if he was…disappointed?

"Whatever you're thinking," he said, "don't. Be brave with me, baby."

The words bolstered her flagging courage and confidence like nothing else could. Inhaling a deep breath, she stepped out of the pool of black lace at her feet and removed her shoes. Though he stood a short distance away, silent as a statue, his tall frame and powerful shoulders seemed to dwarf her. The disparity in their heights was even more pronounced without her stilettoes. Her pulse hammering, she eased the straps of her dress and loosened bra down her shoulders. With one shove of the material over her hips, she was completely naked.

She fought the urge to cover her breasts and sex like some Victorian virgin. And succeeded. But she could do nothing about the blush that scalded her face, neck, and chest. Rion didn't ease her discomfort. His hooded stare roamed every inch of her from her tousled hair, over her breasts and pebbling nipples, down her tad-less-than-flat belly, lingering on the trimmed triangle of hair between her legs, and lower to her bare, unpainted toes. *Say something.* The plea remained trapped behind her clenched teeth, but it ricocheted off the walls of her head. Still, his expression revealed nothing.

No. That wasn't true. When his eyes returned to hers, she almost flinched from the heat. It smoldered like dark, roiling storm clouds. Intense, hot…dangerous.

"On the bed." The low, growled order reverberated in the room and danced over her skin.

Turning, she headed for the large, four-poster bed and climbed onto the mattress, conscious of his attention on the line of her spine, her bared behind, the exposed folds of her sex, and even the backs of her knees. She shouldn't have been able to practically *feel* his scrutiny—fanciful thoughts like that belonged to romance novels and science fiction—but damn if she didn't. It marked her.

She propped up on her elbows and snatched the opportunity to scan the room. Anything to give herself a few moments before meeting that all-too-perceptive stare. The king-size bed dominated the room that was pretty spartan compared to the other places she'd already visited in the club. A huge oak armoire that wouldn't have been out of place in the Beast's castle from *Beauty and the Beast* sat in a corner while two big armchairs flanked a banked fireplace. An ornate lamp on the bedside table provided the only light, but it cast enough illumination for her to glimpse the mural adorning the wall directly behind Rion. Her breath caught. Painted in variations of green, gold, and white, a couple with their arms and legs entwined lay on a carpet of grass. Vines and flowers twisted around their nude bodies in a sensual embrace. It was gorgeous. Magical. And while on the surface too whimsical for this den of sex and hedonism, it fit perfectly.

"Eyes on me," Rion instructed and, unable to resist, she fixed her attention on him. The flutters in her belly morphed into rapid beating, and if she could move, she would've flattened her palm against her stomach to still it.

Dark, intense beauty. Barely leashed power. Seething sexuality. He overwhelmed her.

He stripped out of his jacket and unbuttoned his shirt, revealing inch after inch of taut, golden skin, firm, ripped muscle…and tattoos. Heavy black swirls and stark patterns mixed with dark reds, blues, and purples. He shrugged free of the shirt and tossed it on the chest, revealing that the ink continued over both shoulders and down his right arm to his wrist. The need to study each line and drawing up close, trace them with her tongue, whipped through her. Was it possible to come just from looking at a man? Her tight nipples and damp, clenching sex volunteered a resounding yes. As did her pounding heart.

Jesus, he was beautiful. He stalked over to her and didn't pause until he climbed on the bed and crouched over her like a sleek, faintly menacing, large cat. Muscles danced in sensual tandem under his skin, the display visual foreplay. Unable to not touch him, she flattened her hands over his pecs, stroking down his chest with a low purr she couldn't contain. Slightly ridged flesh scraped her palms. She glanced down, zeroing in on the long, shiny scar of an old wound directly above his abdominals. Three scars, different lengths. Knife wounds. And under her fingertips, hidden by a black wing of a skeletal angel on his shoulder, was a slightly raised circular mark.

Old injuries, wounds. Reminders from his old life.

She sucked in a breath, grief for the pain he must've suffered streaming through her. She'd known it had been rough for him. But apparently he'd hidden just how rough from her.

Rion covered her hands with his. Shifted them to the bed

on either side of her head.

Then he brushed his lips across her forehead.

Her breath snagged in her throat, the gentle caress so… unexpected. Sweet. Reassuring. And it made her heart stutter then beat as hard as it did under his most carnal touch.

A stroke of his mouth over her eyelids, her cheekbones, the bridge of her nose, the line of her jaw, and column of her throat. They left her trembling. Not just with the delicious sensation of his firm mouth grazing over her skin. But in those moments, she felt cherished. As if each whispered caress was a testimony of how lovely he found her. Even in the early days of their marriage, Terrance had never made her feel treasured.

"Stay with me, baby," he murmured against the base of her neck, smoothing a palm down her side and cupping her hip. "Just you and me here."

Trailing a burning caress down the middle of her chest, he slid down her body, and his swirling tongue created a burning path of lust that razed all thoughts from her mind but him and the need he so effortlessly stirred within her. Her nipples ached for his just-shy-of-rough touch, but as he dipped into her navel before continuing lower over her hip, and then… lower…she groaned, tangling her fingers into his thick hair, already hungry for this erotic kiss she'd fantasized about but never experienced.

He slid his hands under her ass, wedging his wide shoulders between her thighs and spreading her wide. Lowering his head, he nuzzled her curls, and she tensed in anticipation, his breath hot puffs of air over her clit.

"Rion, I—"

His tongue licked up her slit.

And she screamed, pleasure a lightning bolt cracking inside her. Her body jerked, and his hard, big hands gripped her hips, holding her still for his mouth. Fire raced up her spine, only to rush back down to the place where he ate her like a starving man. With a groan that vibrated against her flesh, he tasted, sucked, and tongued her, leaving no inch of her untouched. She writhed and twisted under his mouth, a puppet to the erotic strings he tugged and pulled. Feverish cries spilled from her lips when he nipped a fold then soothed it with long, slow laps. Broken pleas tripped from her tongue when he raked his teeth over her sensitive, aching clit, shooting sparks to the base of her spine and back to her spasming sex.

"Goddamn, this pussy is sweet," he growled, rimming her entrance with a blunt fingertip. "Sweet and tight." He sipped at her clit, flicking it, then thrust a finger deep inside her.

Strangling on a scream, she grabbed his head closer, grinding her hips up and down, seeking, begging for each hard stroke. Unlike earlier, he didn't start slow and easy but plunged inside her, the knuckles of his fist bumping her swollen folds with a wet smack that should've been embarrassing but was only hot as hell. Soon, he gave her two, then three fingers, stretching her, igniting a burn that nearly consumed her.

Pushing her legs wider apart, he withdrew then dipped back inside her before trailing a caress along the sensitive skin connecting her sex and ass. She gasped, going still as he probed the crease and circled the sensitive, forbidden hole.

"Relax for me, baby," he murmured. "Don't fight me. Let me in."

Dark, smoky desire curled through her. She shouldn't crave this illicit pleasure, this possession. Good girls didn't. But like Terrance had been fond of telling her, the things she hungered for weren't good. They were dirty. And God, she wanted it. Closing her eyes, she deliberately loosened her muscles, bearing down. When the tip of his finger breached her, she bit her bottom lip but was unable to contain the low, earthy groan that filled the room.

The bite of pain shoved back the arousal for a moment,

but then Rion latched onto her clit, sucking it, tonguing it, and the heat returned in a rush. And when his finger slid deep into her ass, she lifted it into the stroke, crying out. He kept up his raw, sexual assault. One finger, two, rocking inside her.

"Rion," she pleaded. Flames licked at her, created by a taboo touch that filled her like none had before. God, it shouldn't feel this good. She shouldn't feel this…complete.

"That's it," he praised, continuing to thrust in and out of her ass. "I knew you could take this. And you love it, don't you?" A sinful chuckle brushed over her flesh. "Hell yeah, you do. You love having this ass fucked." Lowering his head, he shafted his tongue into her pussy, feasting on her like a man possessed.

She shook, transformed into a wild thing, turned mindless by brutal pleasure. Grunting, he returned his mouth to the top of her sex and drove fingers of his other hand into her pussy.

She exploded. Cracked down the middle and splintered.

Maybe she blacked out. Maybe she died for a few moments before resurrecting to a world re-forged and reshaped by ecstasy. Trembling with tiny mewls clawing at her throat, she came back to herself, her skin as sensitive and raw as a newborn.

Slowly, the shudders eased, her breath softening, leveling out. Only then did she realize the soft brush of lips over her belly. Back and forth. From one side of her stomach to the other.

Oh God.

She blinked, sudden moisture stinging her eyes. With a Herculean effort, she forced her arms beside her rather than crossing them over herself, guarding herself from the tender caresses that threatened to break her in a way his fierce passion and eroticism hadn't.

Her stretch marks.

He was kissing her stretch marks.

She swallowed a sob. Of course he would notice. That perceptive, intense stare didn't miss anything. Neither did he ask her anything. Just worshipped the pale, silvery lines left behind by her pregnancy. Just like the scars that marked his body, permanent reminders of the life she'd lost.

The mattress shifted as Rion stood, leaving her shivering. Moments later, a warm, heavy blanket covered her. She didn't open her eyes, not ready to meet any questions that might be in his. Even when the click of the room door opening then closing reached her, she still kept them squeezed shut.

His searing brand of passion had consumed her. Yet, it was his gentle, almost…loving affection afterward that left her in ashes.

She'd agreed to Rion's terms of walking away after this one night together.

But for the first time since entering the club, she wondered if she would be whole when she did.

Chapter Six

Harper didn't know how much time passed since Rion left the room. Seconds. Minutes. Hours. Lying under the cover he'd spread over her before leaving, she watched the door, instinct deep within assuring her he would return. That they weren't through for the evening.

But what would he want when he reentered? More sex? Or answers. Please, God, don't let it be answers. Tonight was supposed to be about liberating herself, not unburdening her soul. Rion wasn't a dumb man; he would've grasped the significance of the stretch marks. But she didn't speak about Carlie to anyone. Not her parents and not even the grief support group. And here, in this bed, with her emotional skin so thin, so vulnerable, she couldn't discuss her baby with him.

Sighing, she sat up, dragging her tangled hair away from her face. A delicious lethargy from the apocalyptic orgasm dragged at her limbs. Without conscious thought, she rubbed her stomach, the phantom caress of Rion's lips still haunting her. She trembled, still feeling the whisper of his hair across her skin…

The door opened on a hushed *whoosh*. Rion's tall, wide-shouldered frame filled the entrance, his gray gaze immediately finding her on the bed. Black hair tumbled around his face, brushing the dark strands framing his mouth and shadowing his jaw. A knot of lust pulled tight in her stomach, heat winding through her. Just one glance at his masculine beauty, and she reverted to the school girl who'd secretly wanted to pet and stroke him.

So focused on Rion, she didn't notice the figure enter the room behind him. As tall and big as Rion, and light to his dark. Pale blond, closely cut hair. Stark, strong facial bones and a hard but full slash of a mouth that possessed an almost cruel slant. And wolf eyes.

Sasha Merchant.

She jerked her attention back to Rion, who studied her with a hooded stare. Silence permeated the room, the only sound her increasingly rapid, shallow breaths. Understanding dawned, creeping past her shock.

"What's your safe word, Harper?" Rion murmured, stalking closer. Sasha remained near the door, and she could almost feel his intense scrutiny on her face and bared shoulders.

"Rosebud," she whispered, clutching the blanket to her chest.

"Do you want to use it?"

Did she? Part of her screamed a blaring warning to stop, at least slow up. To think. Was she really getting ready to do this? How did she go from being celibate for two years to sex with two men? But then the other half of her reminded her of Rion's stipulation: one night. One night to experience everything she'd fantasized about, everything she had been too afraid and ashamed to ask Terrance for. And if she didn't do this now, she wouldn't. It had to be with Rion, the one man she trusted and desired enough to lead her into this new, intimidating territory. But…

"You don't mind?" When Rion arched an eyebrow in question, she tightened her grip on the blanket. "Sharing me with another man. You don't mind seeing him…touch me?"

An emotion flashed in his gaze, but when he cocked his head to the side, his eyes revealed nothing. "If I said yes, would you go through with it?"

"No." Even though she had no claim on him past the next couple of hours, the idea, the *mere thought*, of his face buried between the thighs of another woman sucker punched her in the chest, the blow swift and bruising. She shook her head. "No, I wouldn't."

He quietly regarded her, his expression as enigmatic as the Sphinx. "Tonight is about pleasure. Yours and mine. And seeing those pretty eyes dilate, hearing you scream my name, and making you come *is* my pleasure. But make no mistake, Harper. He might join us, he might eat your pretty pussy, he might even fill that sexy mouth with his cock, but it will be me giving you what you need. *Me*. So no, I don't mind." He crossed his arms. "Now. Do you want to use your safe word?"

"No," she breathed, the images he'd painted with his words flickering across her brain in a vivid, pay-per-view-only reel. "But…" She hesitated. "Only you inside me. I want… only you."

Once more, something she couldn't decipher flickered in his eyes. Surprise, maybe. But it was darker…fiercer. "Anything else?"

"No."

"Then stand up, and come here," he ordered, his voice deepening, roughening.

The lassitude that had weighted her body disappeared, replaced by a hum that buzzed under her skin like a live wire. Anticipation, arousal, and tendrils of fear twisted and coiled, winding through her veins. Her attention solely fixed on him, she slid across the bed and stood, her feet sinking into the plush carpet.

"Leave the blanket."

Her fingers clutched the cover as if in protest before she dropped it to the mattress and padded over to pause before him. She curled her toes into the carpet and fought the urge not to fidget under two pairs of unwavering gazes.

Rion shifted back a step, then another. Giving Sasha, who hadn't moved from his position against the wall next to the now closed door, a more unobstructed view of her. Dragging her focus away from Rion, she flicked a glance in his friend's direction and clashed with his eerily bright stare. She swallowed a gasp, stunned by the desire burning in that wolf gaze.

"Beautiful, isn't she, Sasha?" Rion murmured to the other silent man, never removing his smoldering regard from her. Over Rion's shoulder, she caught the blond's short nod. Rion continued as if his friend had spoken aloud. "Wait until you taste her. Like honey. Sweet. Thick. Addictive."

She shivered at his description of her sex. At the almost impersonal way he talked about her as if she weren't there. That should piss her off—under other circumstances it would have. But here, with their hot gazes on her, studying her, raking over her breasts and hard nipples, her exposed pussy and quivering thighs…anger was the furthest emotion churning inside her.

"Touch yourself." The demand, though silken, carried an underlying thread of steel. "Go on," he urged. "You touch yourself, don't you, Harper?"

That voice—midnight, tangled sheets, sex, and sin. "Yes," she said, helpless to do anything but answer.

"Are you gentle or rough? Do you rub or circle your clit until it's slippery and aching? Do you slide one or two fingers in your pussy? Show me," he purred. "What do you think about when you touch yourself? What pushes you to the edge?"

You. She bit her bottom lip to keep from spilling that secret, glancing at Sasha, who silently studied her. But why was she hesitant about admitting she envisioned Rion's face? After tonight, it wouldn't matter if he knew. His stipulation granted her a pass to speak her mind without emotional repercussion, because when the morning arrived, she wouldn't see him again. *Keep telling yourself that, sister.* Ignoring the sibilant voice, she met his hooded stare. "You," she confessed. "I think of you."

Rion's mouth firmed, and the skin over his sharp cheekbones seemed to tauten. His eyes… The gray deepened until they almost appeared black with lust and something… wilder. "Then close your eyes and imagine it's my hands squeezing those gorgeous tits and sucking your nipples. Imagine it's my fingers you're coming all over."

Heart pounding, she did as he commanded, not asked. Lashes lowering, she cupped a hand over her breast, and hissed at the pleasure that arrowed straight to her clit, as if a conductor connected the nerve endings. She squeezed her flesh, sliding the other hand down her fluttering belly and between her thighs. Dipping a finger between her already damp folds, she moaned, drawing a lazy circle around her clit and pinching a beaded nipple. Twin darts of electric need shocked her, and she flinched under its lash. *So good…*

"Yeah, it is," Rion rumbled. God, had she uttered the thought aloud? "Harder, baby. Tug on those nipples, rub that pussy. Show us what you like. What you want our mouths and fingers to do to you."

His instructions enflamed her, emboldened her. Casting aside any lingering shreds of modesty or fear, she rolled the tip, tweaked it, loving that he—no, *they*—followed every movement. With a groan, she swept another caress over the pulsing bud at the top of her sex before tracing the wet cleft. The smooth, swollen lips parted under her fingers, and she gathered moisture and thrust deep into her pussy. She gasped, her head falling back on her shoulders. Slick walls sucked at her fingers, and she withdrew, stroking inside again. Lost in the dark arms of lust coiling around her, she edged toward orgasm. Another pull on her nipple. Another polishing rub over her clit. Another hard thrust into her pussy. Another…

A hot, wet mouth closed over the fingers at her nipple while a wide, hard chest pressed to her spine and big, long fingers tangled with hers between her thighs. *Oh Jesus.* Her lashes fluttered open, and she clasped the dark head to her breast, watching his lush mouth draw on her. She cried out as his tongue lashed the aching peak, curling around it and tugging. Another mouth trailed down the side of her neck and over her shoulder even as her hips writhed and undulated under the tormenting strokes to her clit.

Sasha.

Even if her eyes were still closed, she would be able to tell the difference between the two men. Rion's touch had been firm, deliberate, but with a hint of tenderness. Sasha rode his fingertips over the nub in a determined, almost ruthless rhythm that sent bolts of lightning to her clenching sex, lower to her puckered asshole, and zinging back to her clit. He didn't let up, and she couldn't help but think even if she screamed and pleaded, he might not. Not until she shattered. Rion had relentlessly eased her into orgasm; Sasha would catapult her there.

Switching breasts, Rion engulfed her flesh, stabbing the tip of his tongue at the neglected nipple. His fingers plucked and rolled the wet tip, and she bucked under the twin caresses, crying out, digging her nails into his scalp. Closing his teeth over the tendon running alongside her throat, Sasha drove two large fingers into her pussy, and she surged to her toes with the force of it. It was too much. It wasn't enough...

Rion lifted his head, his eyes blazing with lust. "On the bed. Hands and knees."

The heat at her back disappeared, and she stumbled, her legs the consistency of hospital Jell-O. Two pairs of hands shot out and steadied her, one at her elbows, the other at her waist. She stood there for a long second, her breasts, nipples, and sex throbbing in protest of the abrupt departure of mouths and fingers. But one glance into Rion's stern face, and she turned and hustled to the bed. The cool air in the room brushed her swollen, drenched folds as she crouched on the mattress, as he'd ordered. He shrugged free of the shirt he'd slid into before leaving the room and approached the far side of the bed. Sasha remained at the foot, but his hot gaze branded her skin, and she shivered, the weight of his stare causing her clit to pulse. Rion beckoned her with a curl of his fingers, dragging all of her attention back to him. She crawled across the bed, halting when her fingers brushed the edge.

He traced the seam of her mouth, and with a moan, she parted her lips and sucked his finger inside, licking from the tip to the base. She curled her tongue around him, groaning at her first taste of him. Earthy, potent, sinful. A part of her was aware of Sasha, recognized his presence there with them, but at this moment, Rion captured most of her focus, her senses. His flavor and scent overwhelmed her and demanded almost all of her attention.

A low growl emanated from Rion, and he lifted his other hand to her head, tangling his fingers into her hair. "Just like that, Harper. You're going to suck my cock just like that, you understand?" He added another finger, sliding it between her lips, thrusting lightly back and forth along her tongue. "This mouth was created to be fucked," he murmured.

He removed his hands from her and lowered them to his thin, black belt. His slow movements held her mesmerized as he pushed the leather through the buckle, unbuttoned his pants, and lowered the zipper. She glimpsed black boxer briefs before he pulled his erection free.

Holy. *Hell*.

Good God, he was huge.

And beautiful. And intimidating. Long and thick, his cock jutted from a nest of black, coarse-looking curls. The ruddy, almost brutish column tapered into a fat, swollen cap that glistened with drops of pre-cum beading at the small slit. She slicked the tip of her tongue over her bottom lip, already craving the taste of him. Her pussy quivered, clenching in anticipation or anxiety. Probably both. His fingers had been a tight fit. No way in hell could she take all of…that. But damn if her flesh didn't heat and spasm with just the thought of him prying her open, filling her, stretching her until no part of her sex remained untouched. The breath stuttered in her throat. She craved the burn. Wanted it. Just like she hungered for him in her mouth.

"You're staring at my dick like you need it sliding over your tongue and down that virgin throat. Because it hasn't been taken, has it?"

God, no. She shivered as he trailed a fingertip down the front of her neck, his other hand wrapped around the wide, flared base of his erection. Slowly, he slid his hand up the heavy shaft, giving it a healthy, slow pump, the tip disappearing in his fist. When he retreated, his flesh shone with the cum he'd slicked over it. Rion watched her through hooded eyes, as if feasting on her reaction to his stroking himself. Did he see the arousal that set her on fire inside? The damn near desperate need to touch him, lick him, suck him deep? She didn't want to leave here tonight and not have one part of her claimed, marked by his mouth, teeth, tongue, fingers, cock. He could fuck her any way he wanted. She was his.

For tonight, a small voice whispered.

Yes, for tonight.

And if the thought of never again being touched by Rion sliced tiny cuts into her heart, well… She was no stranger to having her heart broken and bruised by him.

"It's mine tonight, Harper," he warned, scraping his nails over her head before gripping the strands in a firm, not-so-gentle hold. She moaned at the minute stings along her scalp, the tiny bites of pain adding to the excitement racing through her on warp speed. "Your mouth, your throat, and anything else I decide to take." With the ruthless hold on her hair, he tilted her head back and shifted forward, the damp tip so close she could catch the tangy, musky, *delicious* scent of the cum welling at the top. He tapped her bottom lip with his flesh, and she couldn't stop herself from licking at the moisture left behind. Her eyes drifted closed, and she moaned, his flavor bursting over her tongue like a sorbet cleansing her palate of all other tastes but his. "Damn," he growled, rubbing the head over her mouth, painting her lips with his cum. "You look so goddamn hungry. For me. Open up, baby. I'm going to fuck this pretty, good girl mouth now."

He pressed forward, and she parted for him, allowing him to breach her. His heavy length slid over her tongue, and she groaned, swirling her tongue around the broad cap and under the flared rim. His moan mated with hers, his hips jerking before he withdrew, leaving her aching and greedy. Once more, two more times, he treated her to those shallow thrusts, granting her just enough of him to tease and work the head and first few inches of him. But the measured strokes weren't enough. God, they just weren't *enough*. She craved what he'd promised. To *fuck* her.

"Please," she pleaded, greed for more of him burning away pride, modesty, and any lingering hesitancy. "Please give me more."

"Do you know what it does to me to hear you beg for my

dick?" he snarled, rolling his hips forward, shafting her mouth with a demanding thrust, surging deeper than his previous strokes. Almost touching the throat he'd been threatening to breach. Whimpering, she stretched her mouth wide, taking more of him, translating without words that he could use her, dirty her, corrupt her. He captured her head between both hands, holding her still for a steady, hard pace. "Do you?" he growled. "Makes me want to give you—" He bit off the rest of the admission, his face set in stark, forbidding lines, his gray eyes gleaming. "Wider. Show me you want more."

Even though her jaw twinged dully in protest, she did as he commanded, and he buried more than half his length in her mouth, the head bumping the narrow tunnel of her throat. As feminine anxiety flared within her chest, the mattress dipped behind her. Hard, large hands cradled her hips, and warm lips brushed over her lower back, then each curve of her ass.

She stiffened, jerking her gaze up to find Rion's on her. His scrutiny roamed over her face as he smoothed a palm over her hair. "Your pleasure is mine," he reminded her… reassured her. It was enough that she relaxed into Sasha's caress, didn't resist his hands spreading her thighs wider.

And when his tongue touched her clit, she cried out, uninhibited, around Rion's cock. His mouth, God, his mouth. It ate at her, feasted. There was nothing gentle or easy about how Sasha tongued her pussy. Voracious, wild. He raked his teeth over the sensitive, pulsing bundle of nerves between her folds, then sucked hard. Sparks cascaded over her senses, and she mewled, the plaintive sound muffled by Rion's flesh. She writhed, unable to decide whether to grind against Sasha's relentless, erotic assault or evade it. Not that he gave her any choice. His big hands held her prisoner, and she could do nothing but accept the probing tongue and lips devouring her.

"Where are you trying to go, baby?" Rion murmured above her, still pistoning inside her mouth. "Play with her ass, Sasha. She loves it. I want her screaming around my dick when I shoot down her throat."

Two blunt fingers thrust inside her pussy, snatching the breath from her. But before her flesh could become accustomed to the invasion, they were gone and slicking a path to her ass. A delicious rumble vibrated over her sex as Sasha rimmed her hole, using her own cream as a lubricant to ease his way inside her ass. The blast of pain. The burn. And then. *Ohhh God.* The ecstasy. The utter pleasure of being stuffed full. Who was she? Who had they turned her into? This creature that desired, pleaded to be pinned, penetrated, and dirtied?

"Hell yeah," Rion grunted. "Every time his finger slides into your ass you suck me harder. Suck it harder. Take it." He glided over her tongue, entered her throat, and she gagged. The channel tightened, instinctively attempting to dispel the intruder. "Easy, baby. Easy. Relax, and breathe through your nose. Don't fight me."

Inhaling, she deliberately loosened her muscles, craving this next invasion, this next possession. And he slipped into her throat with a harsh groan. "That's it. You're so sweet." His fingers flexed against her scalp. "So goddamn sweet. Again, baby. Again."

He withdrew, but immediately pressed forward again, entering the narrow channel and holding still before pulling back. She breathed through the pressure, tears spiking her eyes from both Rion's thrusts and Sasha's greedy mouth eating at her pussy and his measured, firm plunges into her ass. Pleasure raked over her nerve endings with pain-tipped talons. The two of them strung her on a razor's edge, dancing to the erotic tune they played.

With a dark snarl, Sasha lashed her clit, the steady, relentless caress shoving her closer and closer to orgasm. She tried to concentrate on maintaining the rhythm Rion demanded of her, but when Sasha pursed his lips over her and sucked, she surrendered, exploding, shattering. She screamed, just what he'd told Sasha he wanted. Sasha didn't relent, stroking and licking her through it, not letting up until he wrung every shudder and remnant of ecstasy from her.

As if her release signaled his own, Rion growled, and poured a hot stream over her tongue and down her throat. Grunts and low, fierce curses rained down on her, his hips snapping back and forth as he gripped her head tight, keeping her still until she'd sucked him dry. And she did. She drank him down, claiming every drop as her due.

Rion slipped from between her lips, dropping a kiss to her forehead. She shivered, a sigh escaping her. A lassitude inched through her limbs, but before she could surrender to it, two pairs of hands were shifting her, turning her, positioning her so she knelt in the middle of the bed. At the foot of the bed, Rion pushed his pants down his hips and legs, leaving him naked.

Lust punched the air from her lungs.

She'd seen his strong shoulders, wide chest, and sexy, ridged abdomen. She'd studied — and sucked — his gorgeous cock. Now, the animal-like grace and strength of his thighs captured her attention, completing the picture of a man whose face and body could've been chiseled and fashioned by an artist. And like a kid with her face pressed to a candy-store window, she stared at him with awe and greed. Stripped of his clothes, any veneer of civilized had gone away with him. With his chest and abs gleaming with sweat, his still-hard erection flushed and bobbing, here was the wild, fierce beast that seethed and prowled beneath the expensive suit.

All traces of lethargy evaporated as he stalked around the bed and climbed onto it behind her, his legs bracketing hers, his erection riding the crease of her ass, his hands sweeping down the sides of her torso. On a deep growl, he trailed a caress up her torso and cupped her breasts, dragging her back against him.

"I've waited nearly half my life to fuck this pussy, to have you take me into this sweet body. I've wanted to sink balls-deep, just bottom out inside you." He plucked at a nipple, rolling it between his fingers and dragging a whimper out of her. "Tell me you need me there, Harper. Tell me you need me there more than your next breath." Tracing the curve of her shoulder with his lips, he traced a path down her stomach and in between her legs, curling his fingers into her sex still swollen and sensitive from her recent orgasm. He ground the palm of his heel over her clit, and she bucked at his touch. "Tell me, Harper."

"Yes," she breathed, covering his hands with hers, tangling her fingers with his. "I need you. I've always needed you."

Later, she would probably regret that admission. But right now, she just wanted him inside her, filling her past capacity.

A whisper of sound had her shifting her attention to the foot of the bed. Sasha stood there, his wolf eyes on her. With economical movement, he pulled his shirt free of his pants and unbuttoned it, revealing his sculpted, bare chest. She swallowed, her heart thudding against her rib cage as he lowered his hands to his belt, loosened it, and unzipped his pants. Without removing his gaze from her, he pulled his cock free, pushing his pants lower on his beautifully cut hips.

Jesus, to be a part of Rion's circle, was a huge penis a requirement? Sasha fisted a cock that rivaled Rion's in length and width. And almost as beautiful. Almost.

He placed a knee on the mattress, stroking his dick in a grip that seemed punishing.

Rion abandoned her breast and slid a hand up her chest and encircled her throat, his fingers stretching from one side of her neck to the other. Slowly, he rubbed up and down the column.

"You can have her mouth," Rion said to his friend, his voice soft with a hint of bite. "But this," he lightly squeezed her neck, "is mine. You can't come here."

Shock snapped inside her. Possessive. He'd sounded possessive. Of her. Insidious warmth that had nothing to do with the hand casually fingering her sex inched through her. If she tilted her head back, what would she glimpse in his face, his eyes? Afraid to discover the answer, she kept her focus trained on Sasha.

A faint half smile quirked the corner of the other man's mouth, and he seemed unfazed by the threat that darkened Rion's tone. He nodded. "Your woman. Your rules."

Your woman. Her heart executed a stutter step. Sasha probably hadn't meant Rion had claimed her as his own. But her heart was mule-headed. Closing her eyes, she cursed it, reminding the traitorous organ of the bargain that had been set out for their protection.

Rion palmed her inner thighs and spread her legs farther apart, and pressed a hand to the middle of her shoulders. She obeyed the silent command and lowered her torso toward the mattress, placing her at eye level with Sasha's cock. The head shone in the lamplight, his pumping fist pushing a fat drop from the slit. It and the thick vein running along the underside of the wide column called to her. Would he taste different than Rion? *Of course.* The answer was swift, immediate. No one was like Rion.

"Put your hands on his thighs, Harper," Rion instructed, stroking a palm down her spine before retracing the path and cupping her nape. "Suck him deep like you did me." Lips brushed her shoulder, and then his heat covered her back, his arms bracketing her, caging her in. Sheltering her. "Give him the pleasure you gave me. I want this sexy mouth"—his thumb grazed her bottom lip—"to break him."

She shuddered, her sex clenching, her chest heaving as

arousal tangled and twisted within her like a living thing. Power. It beamed bright inside her like a lamp that had just lost its shade. As if it'd always been there, but Rion had removed the shield, had revealed its existence and strength. *Break him*. Rion believed she could bring his dominant, faintly intimidating friend to his knees with pleasure. Like she'd done for him.

The confidence that had been gradually unfurling all evening blossomed into full bloom. Maybe Sasha, with those eerie, piercing eyes, noted it because that small almost smile returned. He dipped his head, possibly in acknowledgment, and slid his hand over her hair, gripping the strands. Both men—Rion, with his hand at the back of her neck, and Sasha with his on her head—guided her toward Sasha's waiting flesh.

Her lips parted around the bulbous tip, and she licked it, savoring his fresh, sharp flavor. Groaning, she dipped her head, swallowing more of him. She teased the fat rim, flicking her tongue under it.

"Goddamn, that's good." He grunted, his grip in her hair tightening, pulling her forward, demanding she take more. God, it was hot—his control…and knowing Rion watched her torment his friend.

Using what Rion had taught her, she hollowed her cheeks, sucking him deep into her mouth, before withdrawing and tracing the vein she'd admired earlier.

"Not a good idea to tease, little girl," Sasha warned, an ominous rumble backing up the advice. Smiling, she followed his order and engulfed him, flattening her tongue, accepting more of him. "That's it, *kotyonok*. Suck this cock."

Deliberate and steady, he buried himself in her mouth, and she loved every stroke. Every glide of his length echoed in her clit like a caress. Yet…when firm lips trailed down her spine, every sense tuned into it. She arched into his kiss, purring like a kitten. Rion, his touch, superseded all others.

For a moment, his body heat disappeared from behind her, but then she caught the dull thud of a drawer opening and closing, followed by foil tearing. Seconds later, Rion clasped her hip while the smooth head of his erection nudged her folds, notching at her entrance.

"Let me in, Harper," Rion murmured, slowly pushing forward, penetrating her. She gasped around Sasha's dick. Rion's big fingers had been inside her, but even they hadn't prepared her for his heavy thickness. Just the tip stretched her, the burn in her resisting flesh stealing her breath. "I want in, baby. If it takes all night, you're going to take me into this pussy. It's mine, and I'm going to have it."

He withdrew, then thrust. Withdrew, then thrust. With every slide forward, he pried her open more, claiming more and more of her for himself. She fluttered and quivered around him, attempting to acclimate to the power and size of him. The pressure ebbed, the minute darts of pain mingling with burgeoning pleasure. God, she'd never been so…completed. So filled beyond capacity that it seemed there was no her or him, but just them melded flesh to flesh.

"That's it, baby," he whispered, reaching around her hip and sweeping a caress over her clit. She cried out, jerked away from his touch that was almost too much with him reshaping her pussy and Sasha pulsing into her mouth. "No," he tsked, rubbing the aching, sensitive nub. "Don't try to run from it. Take everything we're giving you. All of it. It's yours, Harper. All for you."

With a harsh groan, he pulled almost free of her sex then on an air-jacking thrust, buried himself inside her, his balls pressing against the bottom curves of her ass. She screamed, the sound muffled but echoing in the room. Sasha snarled, clutched her head between both hands, and snapped his hips back and forth, driving his erection in and out of her wide mouth.

"Oh yeah." Rion groaned, plunging hard, deep. She writhed, undulating into each drive of his cock. "Your pussy knows me. Knows who it belongs to. Sucking me deep like a hot mouth. Fucking squeezing me tight." Another hard, heavy stroke. "Mine, goddamnit. Mine."

Possessed. They possessed her. Whimpers, groans, and grunts punched the air along with slaps of sweat-drenched skin against skin. The suction of her flesh releasing and welcoming Rion as well as the subtle, wet pop of Sasha's dick surging inside her. It was lewd, carnal, raw. Beautiful.

"So fucking long," Rion groaned. The three words were almost lost beneath the erotic symphony their bodies created, and she barely caught them. But she did. A phantom fist squeezed her heart, the pain and wonder churning with the passion, heightening it, intensifying it.

"I'm about to come," Sasha ground out, lust hardening the warning, and his strokes shortened, roughened. She tightened her mouth, sucking at his flesh like a woman dying of thirst. With a low, animal-like growl, he jerked free, wrapped his fingers around his cock and jacked it in ruthless, brutal pumps. Cum jetted from him, painting his chest and ridged abdomen in streams. A grimace twisted his face, and coarse grunts erupted from his throat.

"You did that to him, Harper," Rion praised, sliding a hand around her throat. "You and that sexy-as-hell mouth."

Cupping the column, he drew her up and back until her spine pressed to his chest. Burying his fingers between her legs, he strummed her clit and rode her, shafting inside her with long, fierce thrusts that had her body singing, reaching for the glimmer of orgasm that loomed so near but just beyond her grasp.

"Please, Rion," she breathed, digging her fingers into his thighs, spreading hers wider so he could have every inch of her. "Please…"

"Let you come?" He placed an open-mouthed, hot kiss along the side of her neck and the crook where neck and shoulder met. "Ask me. Say it, baby. Let me have the words."

"Rion, please. Let me come. I need to come." She didn't care if she begged. The need razing through her, sizzling every square area of skin and firing nerves—she needed relief; she needed him to give it to her.

"That sounds so pretty," he rasped. "Yeah, baby. Give it to me then."

With a sharp, shocking pat to her clit and another stroke, he hurtled her over the edge. Sent her flying. She screamed, convulsing with the almost bruising power of ecstasy. Dimly, she caught his abrupt bark, and his jarring, hard plunges set off another cascade of orgasmic ripples.

As she floated back down and darkness enveloped her, she had her answer to the question that had haunted her earlier.

No.

No, she wouldn't be able to gather the pieces and recognize herself when she left here tonight.

Rion had shattered her, changed her. Shaped her into someone new. Someone stronger, yet vulnerable. Someone confident, yet uncertain.

Someone who was terrified one night with him wouldn't be enough.

Chapter Seven

Rion stared up at the exposed beams in the loft ceiling as if it contained the answers to the egg or chicken's right of primogeniture or the volume of a falling tree in the absence of company.

Get up, damn it. The voice snarled against his skull. The longer he lay in the bed, the scent of sex heavy in the air and listening to the steady, deep rhythm of the dozing woman cradled against him, the harder it became to remember why *this* had to end shortly. Very shortly.

The harder it would become to let Harper walk through the doors of Lick.

Yeah, he had to get up. Get her dressed and out of his club before he did something incredibly stupid and irreversible.

Like beg her to stay.

He shut his eyes, and immediately, images of their night together swarmed in like a hive of angry bees. Harper, bent over the chair in the voyeur room, riding his hand like a jockey racing for the finish line. Harper, deep-throating his cock like she'd never tasted anything better. Harper, sucking his best friend's dick while backing into Rion's, squeezing him with her Saran-Wrap tight pussy.

Harper, whispering that she'd always needed him.

Disgusted, he huffed out a breath. He'd thought he was being so clever coming up with that deadline and stipulation. Thought that by ordering her to leave he didn't have to worry about becoming attached to her and having his heart snatched from his chest again. Thought he was protecting himself.

Trying to be smart, and he'd outsmarted his own damn self.

Now, he faced watching her leave him again. And from the pain clawing at his gut, all his precautions added up to dick.

But the pain let him know he had to do just what he'd initially planned. Let her go. Let her walk out of his life as suddenly as she'd appeared in it. The longer she stayed, the more agonizing the torture of having her turn those sad, dark eyes on him again as she'd done five years earlier. And the deeper the pain of knowing he was no more worthy of her now as he'd been then.

Her husband was dead, and she hadn't searched Rion out for old time's sake. She was slumming it; she'd come to Lick for sex. To her, he was good for getting her off—to give her what he *owed* her—not to build a life with, not to claim him.

Not for forever.

Not that he could give her forever, even if she asked him for it. Back then, he'd been deep into the gang, and now he owned a sex club. He still wasn't someone she could introduce to her parents. And the stink of the streets still clung to him. He, Killian, and Sasha had broken free, but sin still inked his soul, blood still stained his hands. Money and legitimacy didn't make him deserving of her.

Harper nuzzled his chest, splaying her fingers over his nipple. "Did I fall asleep?" she murmured.

Tell her to put her clothes on. She's leaving. "Yeah. Not for long though." He trailed his fingers down her arm then back up. *Damn idiot.* "Are you all right?"

She nodded against him, her tangled hair caressing his skin. He briefly closed his eyes, imprinting that silken sensation to memory. "Yes." A pause. "Thank you."

"For?" Unable to help himself, he tangled his fingers in her hair.

"For making me feel again." Her sigh ghosted over his chest. "It's been a long time since I've felt alive," she whispered.

He hated that—hated that someone as vibrant, as passionate as Harper had been existing instead of living. Hadn't he let her go so she could have security, safety, a perfect life? She deserved to laugh loudly, dance wild and barefoot, fuck with abandon, without fear of condemnation or censorship. What had stifled her? What had stolen her joy?

Terrance. From her confession to him earlier, Terrance had definitely played a part in dousing some of that spirit. But he hadn't been the only one…not the only reason…

He lowered his hand to her belly and traced the thin, pale lines etching her otherwise smooth skin. The marks were fine, silvery, and if he hadn't been kissing her stomach, he wouldn't have noticed the stretch marks. But he had. His heart had lurched. At the time, threads of jealousy had wormed through him, but only for several seconds. Harper had never mentioned a baby. She'd spoken of Terrance but not a child. Which relayed the truth. Because she was the kind of woman created to love, to nurture. And if she had a son or daughter, she would crow with pride. So that left one option…

"Was it a boy or girl?" he murmured.

She stiffened, and he paused, his fingertip resting on a mark just under her navel. The gentlemanly thing would be to let it go. But he'd never been accused of being a gentleman. And some instinct cautioned him that like a festering injury, this particular wound needed to be lanced.

So he waited.

"A girl," she breathed, her body losing none of its tension. "Carlie."

He didn't press her, just let her fingernails dig into his skin as if she were anchoring herself, trying to find purchase in an emotional storm.

She drew a shuddering breath. "Three years ago, I became pregnant. I was overjoyed. I never knew I could be so happy. Terrance and I… Sex between us wasn't often or passionate, but we created this life that I loved from the first moment I saw the plus sign on the test. And he was thrilled, too. The pregnancy actually brought us closer together, and it was a good one. I didn't suffer from morning sickness; I was healthy. She was healthy. And, God, the sound of her heartbeat." She chuckled, the soft burst of laughter leaden with sadness and joy. "A song. The most beautiful song I've ever heard. One I never tired of hearing."

Sliding his fingers along her scalp, he cradled her head, held her to him, sensing the story was veering away from the happiness she described.

"At about seven and a half months, I went to my scheduled doctor's appointment. Like every time, my doctor checked for her heartbeat…but she couldn't find it," Harper rasped. A hard shiver ripped through her, and Rion enclosed his arms around her, brushing his lips over the crown of her head. "I was admitted to the hospital, and they discovered a complication due to insufficient blood flow to the placenta. She…died. Inside me. How, as her mother, didn't I know?" Her voice cracked on a harsh sob. "I still had to give birth to her, knowing I would never hear her first cry, see her draw breath. I cried and screamed through the labor. And when they placed her still, small body in my arms, I died. My lungs worked, my heart beat, but I was dead. I was her mother, but

I couldn't protect her from my own body."

Heartbreaking sobs racked her. As if a plug had been pulled, the tears poured from her in a torrent so vicious, it scared him. He sat up, carrying her with him. Tugging the blanket free from the bed, he set her on his lap and wrapped them both in the comforter. Rocking her, he let her weep, let her cry out her pain, and he held her through the storm.

Once she quieted, he rubbed his chin over the crown of her head.

"When I met you, I was marking time," he said. "I'd made it to my junior year only to spite my father because he kept hounding me about dropping out. See, by the time I'd met you, I already had a juvenile record for larceny and misdemeanor assault. Boosting cars and fights. But my father couldn't have been more proud. To Darry Ward, my education should've been conducted on the streets of the South End, stealing and collecting debts for the gang, not in a classroom. I planned to make it through the first part of the year before quitting. Then you befriended me."

"You mean you stood up for a freshman nerd who was tormented by jocks," she objected with a snort.

"You talked to me in Ms. Dennison's English class. Refused to give up on me."

He hadn't meant to speak to her about his past—about the most joyous and painful part of his life, but she'd opened up to him, shared her soul with him. The least he could do was honor her trust and vulnerability with his. She deserved as much.

"Most girls like you—the ones from the good, safe neighborhoods with two-parent homes and no idea of poverty or crime—only wanted one thing from me. A secret, dirty screw in the backseat of my car or in their basement when their parents weren't home. They damn sure didn't walk down the hall with me or speak to me out in the open for all their friends to see. But you did. Even when I didn't trust you at first and tried to scare you into leaving me alone, you wouldn't. Your friendship...it meant everything to me. I still didn't care about school, but your joy when I aced a test or seeing your face light up with a smile every morning... No one's face, not even my own father's, lit up just because they saw me."

He didn't need to close his eyes to picture the pleasure that had gleamed in her dark gaze when he walked into their classroom. As if she cared that he'd shown up. As if he mattered.

"If not for your gentle encouragement..." He snorted, and she huffed out a soft, wry bit of laughter because there'd been nothing "gentle" about how she'd browbeaten and nagged him about coming to school, studying, and not skipping. "I wouldn't have graduated. I definitely wouldn't have pursued photography, applied to community college, or even admitted I loved it. You convinced me that I was more than my fists. That I had talent... That it didn't make me weak."

Rion grasped her chin and tilted her head up. Her eyes, shadowed and glistening with her spent grief, met his. He rubbed his thumb over the plump curve of her bottom lip.

"I'm the man I am today because of you. If not for your friendship, I would be a soulless bastard fucking up lives for the sake of the mob, or caged in a prison, or dead."

He'd remained active in the gang a year after Harper walked away from him, sinking deeper and deeper. Then Killian had gone to jail, and Sasha had been shot while on a job. He'd already lost Harper to Terrance; he couldn't lose his best friends. He couldn't lose himself. That had been four years ago. It'd taken another two years after he'd made his decision to finally get out of the mob, but he'd never looked back.

"You showed me I could be more, that I *am* more. Before

you, I imagined another path for me, but I didn't have the balls or will to pursue it. You lost your baby, and I can't tell you how much your loss tears at me, just knowing you suffered. But, Harper, you didn't fail. I'm living proof you didn't."

He lowered his head and brushed his mouth over hers.

This intimacy he hadn't allowed himself tonight. Fingering her pussy, tonguing it, and burying himself inside her—he'd surrendered to those temptations, but pressing his lips to hers, breathing in her air, tasting her as they stared into each other's eyes… He'd tried to avoid that closeness, that vulnerability. It reminded him too much of the one and only time she'd given this gift to him. And when he'd had to return it.

Not anymore. He submitted to this pleasure, parting her mouth with his lips, sliding deep, deep, searching, savoring… worshipping. Her delicate hands tunneled into his hair, gripping it. But there was nothing delicate about how she tangled with him, licking at the roof of his mouth, sucking on him as if as hungry for his taste as he was for hers. At first questing, tender, soft, the kiss grew into something wild, wet, fierce.

God, he'd fantasized about this for so long—*years*. And like a starving man with his first sampling of food after a famine, he lost control, feasting on her. Tongues dueled, vied for dominance. Teeth clicked. Their moans filled the room. Never enough. He would never get enough of this, of her.

Mouth still mated to hers, he lifted Harper and placed her back on the bed, immediately settling between her thighs and covering her. She rolled her hips, dragging her drenched pussy over his cock like an open-mouthed kiss. He grunted, thrusting against her so the base of his length pressed to her clit, and his balls to her swollen folds. Legs climbing to his waist, she circled his neck with her slim arms, clinging to him.

Abandoning her lips, he raked his teeth over her chin, down her throat and to the damp valley between her breasts.

On a low, hungry groan, he coiled his tongue around a pale, hard nipple and drew hard on it, lashing it until she cried out, bucking beneath him. He pinched the other peak, tweaking it and tugging.

"Rion." She gasped, grinding that sweet pussy against his dick, bathing him in more of her heat. "Please. Inside me."

"Nothing I want more than to fuck you, baby. Pound myself so deep you feel me tomorrow. And the day after that." He reached over and grabbed one of the condoms off the bedside dresser that he'd thrown there earlier. Quickly, he ripped the packet open and sheathed himself, then returned to her breasts. He pressed the two mounds together, flicked and sucked both tips, making her twist and writhe. Beg. "Put me in. You want this cock, put me inside."

He arched, granting her space between their bodies, his tongue continuing to whip and polish her nipples. She whimpered, wrapping her hand around him and guiding it to her entrance. He hissed as wet flesh kissed the swollen, throbbing head. Then, with a flex of his hips, he was gripped in the tightest, hottest, most perfect pussy.

"Damn, baby. Nothing like it. Nothing." He withdrew, plunged back inside. Gritted his teeth as her sex rippled around him. So goddamn slick, plush. Swearing, he reared back, gripped her ass and held her up for his dick. Served her up to it. "Look at you, taking me, spreading for me, swallowing me like a good girl," he growled. Mesmerized, he watched as he slid between her folds, disappearing inside her pussy, his flesh appearing dark and brutish against her feminine lips. "Fucking heaven, Harper. That's what you are. Heaven."

Falling forward, he curled his fingers over the top of the headboard and slammed into her with hard, teeth-jarring thrusts. From base to tip, she squeezed him, coaxing his cum from him with every quiver and squeeze on his flesh. She cried out, her head thrown back, hips crashing with his, silently pleading for what only he could give. He rode her, pistoning into her again and again, bottoming out in a body created for him. No matter what happened after tonight, it wouldn't change the fact that she was his.

Harper stiffened beneath him, a scream tearing from her lungs and shattering in the air. Her pussy clamped down on him like a vise, and he grunted at the strength of it. Goddamn, she was beautiful in orgasm. Lust tautened her smooth skin across her cheekbones, her features strained with passion. Her lush mouth parted, her dark eyes glazed with passion. Clenching his jaw, he pounded into her, riding her through the release, pushing past her milking muscles even as electric pulses sizzled up from his balls, surged up his spine, and back down to his cock. Once the shudders eased, he let go. He rocketed into her. One. Two. Three strokes. Dropping his hands down to the mattress on either side of her head, he covered her mouth with his, kissing her, needing the taste of her in him.

He erupted, cum shooting from him with breath-stealing power and pouring into the condom. It seemed to go on forever…and an instant. He convulsed, a deep, low growl rumbling from him as he gave her everything in him—his seed, his heart. His soul.

...

"This place is huge," Harper whispered. Yes, she was babbling, but the nerves tap-dancing under her skin, and the fist slowly tightening around her throat incited babbling.

Right now, she faced two options. Jabber or beg him to let her stay, to not end their night together.

So. Babble it was.

Rion nodded, but didn't speak. With a hand pressed to the small of her back, he continued to guide her down the hall and into a large open area dotted with couches, tables, and a tall cross-like structure. The hell? But he didn't grant her time to ask. Pausing before a door that blended into the bare brick wall, he punched in a code on a discreet key pad and twisted the knob.

Ambient lighting flickered on as they moved out onto an iron landing. Shifting his hold to her waist, Rion remained close behind her as they descended three flights of stairs to a large vestibule. Dark blue panels lined the walls along with mounted sconces identical to the ones in The Loft. A beautiful, black chaise lounge rested against one wall, another of Rion's framed photographs hanging above it. An image of the Old North Church enshrouded in shadows. The white of the steeple spearing toward the sky shone like a beacon in the gray, moonless sky. It was lonely, stark, yet gorgeous. A perfect description of the man standing beside her.

"My driver is going to take you home," Rion said, his first words since they'd left the room with the green door. He leaned over and removed a Mary Poppins-esque umbrella from a tall, elaborate stand. God. She shook her head. Every sense had been so focused on him, she hadn't noticed the drum of rain outside. "Are you ready?"

Desperation clawed at her throat, a cry nipping at its heels as she studied his stoic, unsmiling face.

Am I ready? You've changed me so I don't feel like I occupy this body by myself anymore. Like you're now a permanent part of me. So hell no. I'm not ready.

"Yes."

Nodding, he pushed the heavy steel door open and stepped out, popping up the umbrella. Rain sluiced off the sides of the material, framing him in cascades of water. He extended a hand toward her...and she stepped back, farther into the building, shaking her head.

Frowning, Rion lowered his arm and reentered the lobby.

"What's wrong, Harper?"

Her heart thudded against her rib cage, and no amount of swallowing brought moisture to her mouth.

"Harper," he pressed, setting the dripping umbrella on the floor and grasping her upper arms in a gentle, but implacable grip.

"I-I don't want just one night," she breathed. Even as the words exited her lips, part of her longed to drag them back kicking and screaming. But the other part sighed in relief. Because maybe…just maybe…

The concern disappeared from his face, and from one moment to the next, he became closed off to her. A wall slammed down over his features, shutting her out.

"What do you want?" he murmured. "One more? Two?"

Unease slithered through her, twisting in her belly. "I don't know," she lied.

One, two, three nights—she wanted them and more. So much more. Because she loved him. Initially, she'd wrapped up coming to him as lust. But letting him touch her in a roomful of strangers, trusting him to guide her into a ménage à trois…opening her heart to talk to him about Carlie… That had required more than arousal and need. Maybe she'd never stopped loving him. Maybe her feelings had prevented her from giving Terrance all of herself. Maybe…

She couldn't say for certain, because the only thing she was absolutely, 100 percent sure about was this huge emotion pressing against her sternum scared the hell out of her.

Love meant exposing herself to the pain of loss and powerlessness and hopelessness. She'd sworn never to be that vulnerable again. But here she stood, her chest wide open and her heart bare and unprotected. Loving him with everything in her.

God, why didn't he show some emotion? What was he thinking?

"I just... I don't want this to end," she added, silently begging him to hear what she couldn't say. Again, fear bridled her tongue. Fear of rejection.

Fucking heaven, Harper. That's what you are. Heaven.

He'd whispered those words while deep inside her after he'd confessed how she'd changed his life. But never had he mentioned wanting more with her.

Loving her.

Rion stared at her, his gray eyes black in the low lighting and as shuttered as his expression. "For how long?" His eyes narrowed, though his tone remained low, soft. "A week. A month. A year? In that time, am I your dirty little secret? Do you lie to your friends and family about where you spend your nights, about who and what I am? Because God knows I don't fit into your proper, white-washed world. So if this ends—*when* this ends—do we just enforce the stipulation of walking away and not seeing each other again then?"

She shook her head, but the reply lodged in her throat. What was she missing here? Why did he sound angry? No. Not angry. Hurt. Somehow, she'd *hurt* him. When had she ever given him the impression that she was...*ashamed* of him?

"Rion, I—" She stretched out a hand toward him, needing to touch him, comfort him.

"I can't do—" He bit off the rest of the sentence and turned away from her. A muscle ticked along the rock hard line of his jaw. After several moments, he looked at her again, and once more, his gaze seemed carefully blanked. "Listen, you've had an intense night, and I can understand why that would lead you to believe you feel more than you do. But we should stick to our bargain."

Shock slapped at her, and she flinched. "Are you—" She huffed out a brief burst of laughter that didn't possess an ounce of humor. "Are you telling me that because of sex I don't know my own mind?" He parted his lips, but she slammed up a hand. "Never mind. I've had enough of people instructing me on what I mean, what I'm thinking, and what I need. If you don't want me, that's one thing. But please don't patronize me."

Pain and humiliation scored her. She pushed past Rion and shoved open the door, not bothering with the umbrella. In seconds, the rain plastered her hair and clothes to her body, but she didn't feel the wet or the chill.

"Damn it, Harper." His growl reached her seconds before his fingers closed around her arm, jerking her to a stop just as his driver opened the rear door.

He jerked her against his chest, and his mouth crushed hers. With a loud, greedy moan, his tongue speared between her lips, and for a moment, she melted, meeting him thrust for thrust. She whimpered into his mouth, opening wider so he could have more of her.

He doesn't want more of you. Just like five years ago.

The whisper brushed across the walls of her head, and she wrenched free, her breath harsh, serrated by the anguish and hurt that flooded her like a swollen river.

Without sparing him another glance, she stumbled into the car and tugged the door closed, not waiting for the driver. She had to get away from him, from the agony of his rejection, before she did something she regretted.

Like beg him to chase her.

Chapter Eight

"So you're still here."

Swearing under his breath, Rion turned away from his office window and the view of the Leather District at dawn on a Sunday morning. So deep in thought, he hadn't heard his office door open. Or his friend enter.

"You need to wear a cow bell or something around your neck," he snapped at Killian. Damn. It never failed to amaze him how someone so big could move so silently. It was impressive…and eerie.

As Killian moved out of the shadows and farther into the room, Rion didn't bother asking how his friend had spent the night before. The darkening bruise along his jaw and the cut on his bottom lip told the story. More contusions would probably mark his torso, but not many; Killian was damn good at what he did. Another underground fight. Demons rode Killian, and he had two outlets for the rage and pain that seethed under his skin like a boiling cauldron: fighting and fucking. And no woman had caused the injuries to the other man's face. Fists had.

"I work here, don't I?" Rion rounded his desk and leaned against the front, arms crossed.

Killian matched Rion's stance, his feet spread wide, and a dark eyebrow arched high. "Is that how we're gonna play this? Okay." He shrugged a shoulder. "Yes, you do work here. But you don't live here. Which I think you may have forgotten since you haven't left this place since Friday. Now…" He paused, his hazel gaze sharp as a scalpel. And just as incisive. Bastard. "We can dance around why, or you can just tell me why you let Harper leave."

"I'm not talking about her."

"I didn't think shit could surprise me anymore. But seems I was wrong. First, learning from Sasha that Harper Shaw was here at the club. The only girl who's ever had your balls in a twist had walked in here looking for you. Then second, finding out you just let her walk out of here. What the fuck is wrong with you?" Killian snarled, his disgust evident in the curled corner of his mouth.

"Leave. It. Alone. Killian," Rion gritted out.

His friend snorted. "Your gynecologist called. She wanted to set up an appointment for you."

Fury rolled through him, and he launched off the desk, pushing his face into Killian's. "I said, let it go, goddamnit," he ground out.

Instead of shoving Rion away, who loved a good fight, Killian smiled. "So you do give a fuck. I was beginning to wonder."

They stared at one another for the space of several heartbeats before Rion grunted, pivoting around and tunneling fingers through his hair. "I'm not in the mood for your mind games, Killian. Save them for the ring and whatever sorry idiot you're beating the shit out of."

"What are you in the mood for? Getting drunk, maybe? Brooding over how stupid you're being to waste another five years?"

"You don't know—" Rion swallowed the rest of the accusation back. Remorse rushed in. Asshole. He was a grade-A asshole. If anyone understood the agony of lost time, it was Killian. Jail had robbed him of two years of his life. A woman had stolen more than that. "Sorry," he murmured.

Again, Killian shrugged. "Because I do know why I'm in here riding your ass." He lowered his arms and held out his hands, scarred palms up. "You think we don't know how much you loved Harper? That we don't know why you gave her up? Hell, Ri," Killian continued, "how many people get second chances? And here you are blowing it, and for what? What reason could possibly justify letting her walk out of here tonight?"

"*Because she's not for me.*" All the rage inside him blasted out like he'd gone supernova.

Her words hounded at him. And no matter how he tried to turn down the volume, he could hear it over and over. *I don't want just one night.* For a second—for one, blinding, joy-filled second—hope had wrapped its bony fingers around his heart. Then she'd admitted to not knowing how long she wanted him.

Didn't know how long it would be before she decided to stop slumming. One week, one month, maybe even a year. The length of time wouldn't change the result. Her returning to her neat little life that didn't include the owner of a sex aphrodisiac club. He shook his head. What? Would she invite him to dinner with family like their own BDSM version of *Guess Who's Coming to Dinner?* Yeah, her parents accepting him into their tight-knit, proper, and decorous fold was as likely as peace in the Middle East.

No, once more Harper would find a safe, nice guy like Terrance. Once again, he'd know it was better that way, what she needed…deserved. And once again, Rion would walk around like the walking wounded, alive but with a huge, gaping hole in his chest.

After finally savoring her strawberry-and-cream scent on his tongue, after being inside her for hours and being milked by her pussy and perfect mouth, after holding her while she wept, and having tasted her kiss…he was already condemned to nights where he would wake up craving her. Needing her.

Trying to grab onto more time like a desperate fool, all the while knowing it was steadily slipping away, wouldn't ease the pain. Like a surgeon in triage, his only choice had been to sever it before the hurt and loneliness slithered in, poisoning him.

"That's utter bullshit," Killian growled. Rion snapped his head up, and he glared at his friend. Killian returned his scowl, hazel eyes bright with anger. "Bull. Shit," his friend repeated. "If she didn't want you, what the hell were you two doing up here? Playing bridge?"

"That's not what I'm talking about," Rion countered.

"But it's part of it. Sasha told me why she came here. She could've gone anywhere to scratch an itch, but she came to you. Women like her don't fuck and forget. They don't enter into sex easily or without emotion. She searched you out, Ri, after *five years*. What does that say?"

A dismissive answer tunneled up the back of his throat, but it hovered on his tongue. He shook his head. What he wanted her actions to mean and what they actually meant were two different things.

"Damn, open your eyes," Killian said, disgust lacing his tone. "That woman loves you. She always has. You were the one who chose his own insecurities over her."

"The hell are you talking about?" Rion rasped.

Killian's scowl eased, and stuffing his hands in the front pockets of his jeans, he shifted closer to Rion. "If you're honest with yourself, the reason you didn't stop her from marrying that guy then is the same reason you let her go the other night. And it has everything to do with you and nothing to do with her." He paused, and his words sank into the room, embedded into Rion's heart. "You don't believe you're good enough for her. She never believed that; she was your friend when you only had me and Sasha. She was never afraid to walk beside you, and she held her head up high while she did it. She never gave a damn that you were Darry Ward's son. But you…you were the one who never felt worthy. Did it ever occur to you that she might not have gotten married if you'd only opened your mouth and told her how much you loved her? I get it, Ri. You're afraid of being hurt again. But now you have another chance to change both of your lives, and again, you're screwing up."

"What about you, Killian?" Rion murmured. "Knowing the pain that would be waiting for you on the other side, would you still have loved her?"

A shadow flickered in his friend's gaze. "In a heartbeat."

Shit.

Rion blinked. A memory rippled in front of his mind's eye. The same from earlier that evening. Him, walking into his high school English class, searching out and spotting Harper in the second seat in the second row. A bright, happy smile widening that too-lush-for-a-teenager mouth. Then another image wavered, replacing that one. Years later, sitting in a diner across from the Boston University campus. Her, dark brown eyes solemn and wary, telling him she'd accepted Terrance's proposal. As if waiting for him to say something… anything. Waiting for him to stop her.

But he rejected the image even as his stomach tightened with nausea. Because again, he was going to do what was better for her rather than what he wanted.

He met Killian's stare, resolution a heavy weight bearing down on his chest. "I get what you're saying. I do. But…" He paused, clenching his jaw before continuing. "It's because I… care for her that I know I need to let her go."

Anger flared in Killian's hard gaze. "In all your knowing, did you consider that maybe it should be her choice about what's best for her life?" He didn't wait for Rion to reply, but stalked out of the office, not even bothering to slam the door shut behind him. Somehow the soft click was more of an indictment on his opinion of Rion's decision than a resounding boom would've been.

Silence permeated the room. But he wasn't alone. Memories, from years ago and two days ago, crowded in the room. He closed his eyes, savoring the mental reel, acknowledging they detailed the most joy-filled, content moments of his life. He greedily hoarded them because he also understood they would probably be all he had.

Sighing, he opened his eyes, and his gaze landed on his desk. Unbidden, the image of Harper bent over, palms flattened to the surface, her dress hiked around her hips, baring herself to him, wavered and solidified in front of him.

She'd been nervous, maybe even a little terrified—of rejection, of him, of herself and the needs that had brought her to Lick. But she'd also been brave, facing her own fears and insecurities. Honest, giving him the truth, knowing there was a possibility he could use her vulnerability against her. Forgiving, coming to him even though he'd hurt her in the past. And so generous with her reaction to his touch, her pleasure, her body…her heart.

A line from a song he'd heard echoed in his head. Something about a person being who they loved, not who loved them. If that was true, then he was brave, honest, forgiving, and generous. Worthy.

He shuddered.

Now the question was…could he believe?

Chapter Nine

Spending the second night in a row at her parents' house should officially qualify Harper for spinsterhood. But, Saturday had been dinner, and tonight was for a party. Yes, all women attended, and they were gathered together to celebrate her cousin Sylvia's engagement, but there was food and music…so maybe she wasn't as pathetic as she seemed.

Nah. She should stop by the pet store on the way home and adopt her first cat now.

Hell. Was it possible to annoy herself?

"What's all the sighing about, sweetheart?" Raquel Shaw bumped the refrigerator door closed with her full hip, another tray full of antipasto in her hands. "That has to be the fourth one I've heard since you came in here to help." Her mother aimed a pointed look at the coconut pie she'd charged Harper with slicing…that had only one cut in it. "What's wrong?"

Oh nothing. I just can't figure out a way of performing an emotional lobotomy to scrub away the memories of the man I love fucking me then leaving me. Somehow she doubted that admission would go over smooth with her mother, so Harper stuck with shaking her head.

"Sweetie." Her mother set the tray on the butcher block island and slid an arm around Harper's waist, squeezing. "Is this too hard for you? Being here? Sylvia worried it might be…"

"No, Mama." Harper hugged her close. "I'm okay, I promise. Please stop worrying."

The mother-henning could be a bit smothering at times. But Harper never doubted her mother's love. Her and her father's affection and protection had been a constant in her life. After Carlie and Terrance's deaths, Harper had leaned on it. Often. They'd seen their daughter at her worst, and so now that Harper was trying to find her independence and "sea legs" again, they were there, their arms stretched out, ready to catch her if she stumbled. Even if Harper wanted to scrape her knees a few times.

"Asking me to stop worrying is like telling me to stop breathing. You're my baby." She cupped her cheeks and smacked a kiss on Harper's cheek before patting it and turning back to the appetizers. "You know…"

"Oh God." Harper groaned.

"Shush it. Don't use the Lord's name in vain," her mother admonished. "Now, as I was saying. One reason I'm glad you came tonight is so you can see that even though life holds tragedies, it also brings happiness. Like your cousin. Sweetie, there will be another Terrance out there. You just have to be ready to receive him. You can't allow grief to close your heart to love or a family."

Harper closed her eyes, the knife hovering above the dessert, trembling. The Band-Aid she'd slapped over her heart loosened, and the cracks zig-zagged wider. "What happens when you open your heart, and the person you offer it to doesn't want it?"

Her mother stilled, and chatter from the living room

filtered into the silent kitchen. With deliberate movements, she wiped her palms on her apron and lowered to a stool. Folding her hands in her lap, she studied Harper with the dark brown gaze she'd passed down to her.

"Spill," her mom ordered.

Cursing her wayward mouth, Harper covered the coconut pie with a sheet of plastic wrap and settled on the matching stool.

"When I told you last night that I'd spent Friday evening with friends, I wasn't being exactly truthful," Harper confessed.

Her mother arched a black eyebrow. "Exactly truthful? That's like being a little pregnant. Either you lied or you didn't."

"Okay, I was with an old friend. Not plural," Harper hedged.

"And is this *friend* the one who has you sighing and moody because he broke your heart?"

"Yes," Harper murmured. "But in his defense, he doesn't know he has my heart to break."

"Well that's two strikes against him already," her mother huffed. "One, that he hurt you, and two that he doesn't have the sense God gave a goat to realize there's a beautiful woman right there who loves him. Who is this *friend*?"

"Mama." Harper smiled, briefly squeezing her mother's hands. "He's…" She hesitated, memories of how her parents had disapproved of her friendship with Rion in the past, giving her pause. "He's not like Terrance."

She waved a hand. "Well, of course not. But you can't constantly compare other men to him…"

"I'm not." There wasn't a comparison. "Mama, I loved Terrance. Overall, he was a good man, a provider, and he would've been a wonderful father. In the beginning, he made me feel safe, secure, but even if he had lived, I don't know if we would have stayed married."

Astonishment widened her mother's eyes and parted her lips on a soft gasp. "Harper."

"It's true, and it hurts me to tell you this because I know how much you and Dad loved Terrance. Even in the short amount of time we were together, we started to drift apart. It started before Carlie, but widened further after we lost her," she said.

For the first time since the doctor had delivered the news about her baby's death, Harper uttered her daughter's name with ease. As if her cathartic confession and grieving with Rion the night before had ripped the scab off the wound so it could start to heal properly. Oh, the pain still existed, but now she could say her baby's name without feeling as if shards of glass scraped her throat raw.

"Her death damaged something with us that already wasn't strong enough to withstand a blow." Harper forced herself to meet the dark eyes so like her own. "Terrance…hurt me." At her mother's soft and outraged gasp, Harper quickly covered the other woman's hand with her own, squeezing tightly. "Not physically. He never lifted a hand toward me, but emotionally. He could be cold, distant…critical. I wanted the affection and easy love that you and Dad have, but instead I was lonely, hungry for intimacy, for…acceptance. Terrance may have provided a home, clothes, and food… He may have given me financial security and safety, but my heart wasn't safe with him. He wounded me in a way that made me not just doubt my femininity, but ashamed of it. He *hurt* me." Repeating the words were cathartic, an affirmation of the truth. Of the fact that he should've cared and loved all of her, not made her feel dirty for her desires and needs. That he'd been wrong. Not her.

"I'm so sorry, sweetheart. I thought you two were happy. I didn't see…" her mother whispered, her voice faltering as moisture glistened in her eyes. "I'm so sorry I didn't see."

Harper expelled a heavy—cleansing—breath. "You have nothing to apologize for, Mama. And it's okay; *I'm* okay. Really." And she was. She could admit the true state of her marriage and not feel as if she'd been rubber-stamped with failure. "Also, now I can admit I married Terrance for the wrong reasons. Instead of running to him, I was running from someone else."

Her mother studied her, understanding dawning. "You were in love with someone else," she whispered. "But who…" Shock whipped across her expression. "Not the Ward boy."

"His name is Rion, Mama. Rion Ward. And yes, him."

"Oh, Harper," she breathed, already shaking her head.

"No," Harper said, holding her hand up. She didn't want to be disrespectful to her mother, but she also couldn't let her say anything negative about Rion, either. Yes, every time she dwelled on him sending her away the night before last—which occurred every three minutes—her body throbbed in pain, but he was a good man. His one, glaring flaw was that he didn't love her. "You don't know him. Not like I do. I understand why you and Dad didn't approve of him. I didn't then, but now, I do. In your shoes and with my child, I might've felt the same way. But he was—*is*—so much more than where he came from. He's a protector with an artist's heart. He wasn't given anything in life but a hard time, but he refused to let it define him, and he is now a successful businessman. He's honorable, kind, driven, and if you're lucky enough to be called his friend, he's fierce and loyal. And I've loved him since I was fourteen."

Her pulse raced at her throat like a horse at the crack of a shot.

She'd loved Rion with all the angsty passion of a teen and later with the hungry desire of a woman. Even when she'd tried to put him from her mind and heart, he'd just burrowed deeper. Five years ago, she'd delivered an ultimatum, and had lost. And last night, fear had stilled her tongue again.

Trust was the biggest risk. Going to Lick had been about coming alive again. She was never more alive than when she was with Rion. Not just the sex, but him. *He* made her alive. "I don't want to live the next five years like the last. Without him," she murmured to herself.

"Raquel, Harper, we're star—" her aunt Lydia chirped, sailing into the silent kitchen. She skidded to a halt, her wide gaze darting from her sister to Harper. "Uh. Everything okay in here?"

"Fine," her mother said, not removing her quiet scrutiny from Harper. "We're fine and will be there in just a few minutes."

"Okay." Another quick glance between the two of them, and her aunt backed out the kitchen entrance. Probably to regale the women in the living room with tales of tension and strife between Harper and her mother. She loved her aunt, but the woman was the biggest gossip. "I'll see you"— she jerked her thumb over her shoulder—"in there."

"Good Lord," her mother grumbled, easing off the stool. "We need to get in there; otherwise, she'll have that whole room believing we were in here rolling in the antipasto."

Snickering, Harper followed suit, tugged back the wrap on the pie, and quickly finished cutting the dessert into slices. As she lifted the platter, a gentle hand on her arm stopped her.

"I love you, Harper. And all your father and I ever wanted was your happiness." Not waiting for her reply, she picked up the tray of appetizers and headed into the party. Harper stared after her mother, but then after several seconds, smiled. And joined the party.

An hour later, when the trays of food had been plowed through, the games had been played, and Sylvia wore a veil of tissue paper, ribbons, and bows from the gifts, the doorbell rang. With the raucous laughter filling the room—courtesy of Lydia's "special punch"—Harper almost missed it. Before she could make a move to answer it, one of her cousins had already leaped up—a pretty impressive feat considering she'd drunk at least three cups of the punch—and disappeared down the hall.

Moments later, she reappeared in the living room entrance, wearing a shell-shocked expression.

"Um, Harper. It's for you."

"What are you..." She slowly straightened, the bingo cards from the Meet the Bride and Groom game tumbling from her fingers as a tall figure stepped from behind her cousin.

Rion.

His gray gaze scanned the room, and she waited, breath trapped in her throat, for the moment he found her. And when he did...

God.

The heat. It turned his eyes molten, and from the amount of gasps and sighs in the room, she wasn't the only one who noticed it.

Uncaring if her family later called her a shameless hussy, she drank him in. Thick, black hair waved back from the sharp, clean lines of his face, drawing attention to his masculine beauty. The dark hair shadowing his jaw and surrounding the sinful curves of his mouth only added to the aura of strength and sensuality that clung to him.

It'd been two days since she'd stroked that powerful, lean body. Since he'd kissed her. Made her body scream. Hell, made her scream.

Those days might as well have been years. Need rolled through her like a steam engine. Her arms ached to wrap themselves around him. She longed to inhale his earthy scent. But the memory of rejection, of the pain he'd inflicted, held her frozen. Glued her feet to the floor.

"Excuse me, ladies, and please forgive me for intruding," he said, his deep, sex-and-sin voice like a physical caress.

"It's okay," one of her cousin's bridesmaids purred.

Harper shot a glare in the woman's direction. It would be a shame if Sylvia's bridal party was down one person.

"Harper." He held a hand out to her, and another chorus of sighs rose in the air. "Can I speak with you, please?"

She stared at his upturned palm, shock still not ready to turn her loose. Rion stood in her parents' home. Looking for her. Surely if she pinched herself, she would wake up in her bedroom, shivering, some paid program droning away on the television.

So don't pinch yourself. Keep your hands to yourself, a voice urged. Because if this was a dream, she didn't want to wake up.

"Harper?" he pressed.

"Yes," she breathed. Wending a path through the enthralled women, she approached Rion. And, after a moment's hesitation, slid her hand over his. Long, elegant fingers enclosed around hers, and she trembled. Remembering. Wanting. Just what she'd wanted to avoid. Yes, she'd admitted to herself that she loved him. But that didn't make her a doormat. She wanted all or nothing with Rion. And if he couldn't give that to her—wouldn't give that to her—then after he said whatever he'd come here to say, she'd still love him, but she'd also walk away.

Silently, she followed him back down the hallway and out the front door. The warm September night air wrapped around her like a comforting blanket, but did nothing for the somersaults transforming her belly into a trampoline.

Speak. Say something. But she couldn't force a word past the emotional noose strangling her. Why was he here? Why had he come after her when the last thing he'd said to her was something about sticking to their one-night agreement?

"Thank you for seeing me, Harper." He slid his hands in the pockets of his black pants. "I wouldn't have blamed you if you refused."

"How did you know where to find me?" Out of all the questions brewing and whirling in her head, this wasn't by far the most important but the first one that popped out of her mouth.

He studied her, a faint smile quirking a corner of his mouth. "We have an investigator on staff. Finding your home address wasn't hard. I went there first, but when you weren't home, I remembered where your parents lived and chanced coming here."

"An investigator?" She shook her head. "That could be considered stalking in some states."

His smile deepened. "Probably." His lips firmed, straightened. "I needed to see you." He studied her, silent for a long moment. "Harper, I'm sorry about how I let you leave."

That quick the flicker of hope wavering in her chest—fucking, stupid hope—sputtered and died. Oh. He'd sought her out to make sure she was okay, that she harbored no hard feelings.

Like a friend would do.

Jesus. How many more pieces could a heart break into?

"It's fine. *I'm* fine," she lied, battling back the moisture that stung her eyes. "You didn't need to go through so much trouble for that." *No tear is going to fall, damn it.*

"No, it's not fine," he said, his tone hardening, that too-perceptive gaze searching her face. She longed to duck her head, avoid his scrutiny. But she met his eyes and prayed he didn't notice the pain that churned inside her. "I shouldn't have let you leave thinking I didn't want you. That I didn't need you. You should never question how much you're desired, and for me to let you go doubting was a sin."

Warmth, like a tight embrace, squeezed her. Soothed a cooling balm on her battered feelings and pride. Believing he could so easily dismiss her after a night that had rocked the foundation of her world had hurt. While she'd allowed herself to think the passion they'd shared had been special, he'd sent her away as if it had been par for the course. Even if he couldn't love her, his words helped ease the pain.

"Thank you," she murmured, meaning it.

"That's not the only reason I'm here." The thick fringe of his lashes lowered, hiding his penetrating stare from her. And for the first time, she noticed the faint smudges under his eyes. As if he hadn't slept... She frowned, but a moment later, his gaze pinned her in place like a butterfly trapped on a corkboard, and the thought passed out of her head. "I love you."

Shock doused her, the frigid blast pummeling the breath from her chest. She hadn't heard... He hadn't said... *What?*

He growled, thrusting a hand through his hair. His eyes narrowed on her. "I don't have pretty words. I never have. If I did, I might have said them years ago. But before you and since you, I've had no use for them. All I have is the bare, sometimes ugly truth."

Several seconds passed where he turned and seemed to contemplate their neighbor's front lawn with the Fourth of July flags they'd yet to take down. Impatience, fear that she'd somehow misunderstood him, and that stubborn hope surged within her, filling her like hot air, and pressing against her sternum. Finally, he returned his gaze to her, and she barely stifled a flinch at the raw intensity darkening it.

"I realize there were sixteen years of my life when I didn't know you, but still, it doesn't seem like there wasn't a time when I didn't love you. Yes, I've always wanted you. Wanted to kiss you, slip my hand under those short plaid skirts you loved, touch you, and make you look at me with something more than friendship. But that need always came second. More than feeling you come around my fingers, I wanted your heart. Your devotion. Your present and your future. I wanted *you*."

He lifted his hand, studied the wide palm, the long fingers. "I came to you as a boy whose hands were already stained with blood, who'd already dished out pain and had been scarred by it. I was a thief, a thug. You saw that but so much more. To you, I wasn't the troublemaker on the edge of dropping out or the gangbanger to fuck in the backseat of a car. I was worth something to you, and I loved you for that. Even to my father and the gang, I had to prove my worth, but you accepted me as is and made me believe I could be so much more. Still, I never felt good enough for you. In my heart, I thought your parents were right to warn you away from me. As much as I ached with the need to touch you and wanted to make love to you, take what you offered me, these criminal's hands had no right. I had no right to drag you into a life that wasn't a life. One where you could be hurt or worse because of me. Letting you go, not telling you not to marry Terrance was one of the hardest things I've ever done. But, in my mind, stopping you from having everything he could give you would've been selfish on my part. You were worth that sacrifice."

"Rion." She didn't bother suppressing the tears now. Not when they were for his pain rather than her own. Crying for him seemed just since this strong, stoic man wouldn't do it for himself.

He shifted closer, erasing the small amount of distance between them. The hand he lifted to her face trembled. And it shattered her.

"Rion." She shook her head, covering his hand with hers. "I can't… I don't know if I can do this again. I don't know if I'm strong enough. I'm tired of being hurt…"

"Harper, please," he murmured, stroking a thumb over

her cheek. "Just, please, listen to me, baby, okay? I insisted on that one-night stipulation to protect myself. I was scared. Scared to open myself to the pain of losing you. It damn near destroyed me five years ago, and I couldn't go through it again. But I also couldn't pass up the chance to be inside you, taste you, claim you. I'm a selfish bastard, and if I couldn't have your love, I could at least have that. I sent you away because I believed my life was no place for you. Yes, I'm out of the gang, but the club, The Loft… Though legal, I didn't think it was where you belonged. Didn't think it was something you wouldn't be ashamed of… Didn't think I was someone you could be proud to claim." A muscle flexed along his jaw. "But after two days of not seeing you, not touching you, holding you, I don't care. I don't have the power, the will to stay away from you any longer. I can't stop thinking about you. Smelling you on my skin. Needing you. I don't want to stop."

Even as fledgling hope fluttered in her chest, she stepped back, anger rolling up through her. "For more years than I care to admit, other people have told me what's good for me, what I need. I came to your club to break away from that, to take control of my life. And you don't get to take that away from me. You don't get to say what I deserve or need. You don't have the right to decide any of that. Only *I* do. As for being ashamed of you?" She glared at him, furious, before marching past him and up the front steps. Throwing open the front door, she called out, "Mama, could you come here, please?"

Moments later her mother appeared in the hall and cautiously approached the doorway. Behind her, the other women gathered in the living room entrance.

"Harper?" she murmured. "Is everything okay?"

"Yes." Tossing a scowl over her shoulder, she stepped aside. "Mama, you remember Rion Ward? Rion, this is my mother, Raquel." Introductions done, she turned to her mother, briefly glancing back into the house. "Mama…Aunt

Lydia, Sylvia, if he finally gets it through his head that I make my own decisions, Rion could possibly be my boyfriend. He also owns a sex club that empowers women. No strippers. Okay?"

Eyes wide, her olive skin paling, her mother nodded. "Okay," she whispered.

Behind her, Lydia, Sylvia, and the other guests gaped. Harper gave it five seconds before this hit Facebook.

"Great. I'll be in shortly." Gently, she closed the door and retraced her steps, returning to Rion.

He stared at her, a half smile quirking a corner of his mouth. "I can't be sure, but I think your mother made the sign of the cross as you closed the door."

Yeah, Harper had caught that, too. But, she'd get over it. Or maybe not. It didn't matter, as she'd told Rion, this was her life, not her parents'. She hoped they accepted Rion, but if they didn't… Well, they would love her regardless, that she didn't doubt.

"I'm sorry," he said, voice soft…tender. "For taking your choice away from you. For projecting my own insecurities on you."

"Rion." She shook her head, awed at how he couldn't see how he was…everything. "You were always good enough to me. You're strong, honorable, honest, a protector. I never doubted what and who you were…who you are."

Rion lifted a hand, cupped her cheek. "Don't give up on me now. Please. Tell me again, baby. What you said before you left Friday night. Tell me again."

She didn't need to think about his request. Not when she'd been replaying that night on an endless loop inside her head. "I don't want just one night."

"Whatever you need, baby," he murmured, pressing his forehead to hers. His eyes closed, and she tasted his kiss—mint, fresh rain, *him*—on his breath. "One week. One month.

One year," he swore, repeating his words from the night before. "However long I can have you, I'll take. Every second is worth the risk. *You* are worth the risk."

His mouth covered hers, and she parted for him without hesitation, without holding back. He licked at her tongue as if in question, and when she tangled with him, he moaned, deepening the mating of mouths, lips, and tongues. It was tender, sensual, a promise.

And it was a gift. Just like the man standing before her.

"I love you, Harper." He brushed a kiss over her temple. As if he couldn't resist touching her.

"I love you, too," she whispered, sliding her arms around his neck and burying her face against the strong column. "I always have. I suspect I always will."

"Say it again. I need to hear it. I suspect I always will," he said, giving her own words back to her.

Tipping her head back, she pressed her mouth to his. Tasting him again, still not quite able to grasp that this man—this brooding, sensual, powerful, intense, and beautiful man—belonged to her. Loved her.

She brushed her lips over his one last time.

"I love you." She smiled. "Now I believe there are some rooms left in that Loft of yours that I didn't get a chance to explore."

Amusement lightened his eyes, and the corner of his mouth quirked. "On one stipulation."

She groaned. "Another stipulation? Aren't you tired of those?"

"Just one," he murmured. "At the end of the night, you stay with me."

Joy swelled in her chest. Cupping his face in her hands, she stared into his beautiful face, and once more, blinked back tears.

"Deal."

Acknowledgments

To my Father, who makes all things possible. Thank You for being limitless and for Your faithfulness even when I haven't been as faithful. You are my everything.

To Gary. You took a leap of faith on me, and I don't have the words to express how much your love and sacrifice humbles and strengthens me. You're the best husband, father, and friend God could've blessed me with. And I'm just so thankful He did. Love you.

To my family. I've never known what it's like not to have your support, encouragement, and love. You've been my biggest and loudest cheerleaders, and I love you so much.

To Jessica and Dahlia. We need our own television show. Call it something like Sisterhood of the Traveling Coffee and Word Challenge. Lame? Okay, but this is short notice. LOL! Thank you for the writing challenges that helped get this book written. You two ladies are wonderful, and I'm looking forward to drinking more death-defying coffee and writing more books with you! And Dahlia, thank you for the glimpse into the world of secret sex clubs. Dang, we should've known each other in college! LOL!

To Debra Glass. Thank you for always being willing to read, critique, and advise me. This journey wouldn't have been the same without you. For one, it would've been a helluva lot scarier and uncertain. You've been that calming voice when I needed it, and that ride-or-die chick when I needed that, too. *snicker* Love you, woman!

To Tracy aka Super Editor. Seriously. T-shirt. With a big ol' E in that octagon, diamond thing. I never was good at geometry. LOL! Thank you for believing in me. I swear, if you saw a submission for a haiku poem, you would encourage me to submit, telling me you know I could do it… Even though both of us know with my penchant for wordiness and repetition, it would be an epic fail… LOL! You've challenged me, pushed me, and with every step, bolstered me. I've grown because of you, and thank you isn't enough. You're not just my editor, we're a team. And thank God you're the more rational, experienced—and as much as it pains me to admit—more sarcastic captain.

Lastly, thank you to the Saints and Sinners! You ladies make it a joy to go online every day. Thanks so much for your abounding, more-than-a-little raunchy, crazy, and funnier than hell support! Love y'all!

About the Author

Naima Simone's love of romance was first stirred by Johanna Lindsey, Sandra Brown, and Linda Howard many years ago. Well, not that many. She is only eighteen…ish. Though her first attempt at a romance novel starring Ralph Tresvant from New Edition never saw the light of day, her love of romance, reading, and writing has endured. Published since 2009, she spends her days—and nights—creating stories of unique men and women who experience the first bites of desire, the dizzying heights of passion, and the tender, healing heat of love.

She is wife to Superman, or his non-Kryptonian, less bulletproof equivalent, and mother to the most awesome kids ever. They all live in perfect, sometimes domestically challenged bliss in the southern United States.

Come visit Naima at www.naimasimone.com.

Also by Naima Simone…

Witness to Passion

Killer Curves

The Bachelor Auction series

Beauty and the Bachelor

The Millionaire Makeover

the Secrets and Sins series

Secrets and Sins: Gabriel

Secrets and Sins: Malachim

Secrets and Sins: Raphael

Secrets and Sins: Chayot

If you love erotica, one-click these Scorched releases...

SHAMELESS
a *Playboys in Love* novel by Gina L. Maxwell

People say I'm shameless. They're right. I like my work dirty and my sex even dirtier. It takes a hell of a lot to tilt my moral compass, and dancing as a private stripper for horny suburbanites doesn't even register. Until I meet the one girl in all of Chicago not interested in dry jumping my junk. I know her darkest fantasies. I want her. Bad. Now I need to show her how good it can feel... to be shameless.

DESIRING RED
a *Dark and Dirty* tale by Kristin Miller

Choosing a werewolf mate who'll be with me until I croak? Pardon me while I take some time to think on it. But a steamy encounter before the final ceremony changes everything. Reaper, the Omega's eldest grandson, is fiercely loyal, scorching hot, and built for pleasure. I've only just met him, but I *need* him like no other. By pack law, Reaper can't have me until the Alpha makes his choice...but Reaper's never been one to follow the rules.

LEARNING CURVES
a novella by Cathryn Fox

When he wins a sexy bet, billionaire Linc Blair can't wait to get Lauren Neill naked. He's never gone for her type in the past, and he's pretty certain it has more to do with her buttoned-up hotness than the nagging sense that something is missing from his life. But when he gets a glimpse of the vulnerable woman beneath the conservative, yet oh-so-sexy clothes, it's a game changer.

CPSIA information can be obtained
at www.ICGtesting.com
Printed in the USA
BVHW081214111120
593051BV00002B/217